Gail Hamilton

Nursery Noonings

Gail Hamilton

Nursery Noonings

Reprint of the original, first published in 1875.

1st Edition 2024　|　ISBN: 978-3-38538-302-9

Verlag (Publisher): Outlook Verlag GmbH, Zeilweg 44, 60439 Frankfurt, Deutschland
Vertretungsberechtigt (Authorized to represent): E. Roepke, Zeilweg 44, 60439 Frankfurt, Deutschland
Druck (Print): Books on Demand GmbH, In de Tarpen 42, 22848 Norderstedt, Deutschland

CONTENTS.

NURSERY NOONINGS.

I.

THE BABY IN BREECHES.

THAT "the baby" should be in breeches at
all was owing to the other baby. There was
no call for that baby. There were babies
enough before. When, as breakfast drew near
its close, Harry was heard thumping slowly
down the stairs, pit pat, pit-pattering through
the parlors and the library, and presenting
himself at the dining - room door in fresh
white frock and radiant face, emitting angelic
war whoops of delight, the old house seemed
full of babies. When he rushed around the
room with fixed eyes, bent head, and shoulders thrust forward in frenzied eagerness for
a chair, and when he made good his divine

right to a seat at the table by pushing his
chair headlong into a place regardless of what
broadcloth or ruffles might interpose; when
he had painfully climbed up into the adult
chair and brought his precious nose very nearly to a level with the table—with what serene
delight, with what entire self-approbation and
world-satisfaction, did he gaze around upon
us, his aspiring, ambitious, unsatisfied elders!
With what sweet frankness he poked his sudden fingers into the peach preserve! With
what sublime abstraction did he upset all the
cups and saucers in his endeavor to reach the
oranges! What a small thing it seemed to
him, in flashes of adventurousness, to rise in
his chair, climb up on the table, and creep
along to the otherwise unattainable sugar-
bowl; and when a blind and unreasonable
prejudice interfered with this, his simple and
honorable ambition, what hearty howls attest-
ed his keen sense of right to life, liberty, and
the pursuit of sugar, till some true friend,

more open to conviction than his bigoted pro-
genitors, set the sugar-bowl on the floor, and
restored the equilibrium of the universe!

Certainly Harry was baby enough to satisfy
a reasonable mind. His ignorance was of the
most approved pattern, and penetrated every
fastness in the whole province of knowledge.
He not only, like Sir Thomas More, did not
know Greek at three years of age, but he was
very imperfectly acquainted with English.
He had never so much as heard whether there
be any alphabet. He knew how to tumble all
the collars, ribbons, and trinkets out of the upper drawer into a kaleidoscopic confusion. He
could toss Billy the fireman toward the ceiling
in such eccentric orbits that he would be sure
to strike against the vase and upset the flowers
on his way down. But of any useful knowledge, or of any knowledge that promised to be
useful, he was destitute to a degree that would
have charmed the heart of the most devoted
believer in vital statistics.

But another king arose who knew not Joseph. Another baby must needs come peering and prying into the world, and Baby Harry must abdicate. The badges of his royalty must go. All his little cambric flounces, all his lovely silken-stitched flannel petticoats, the folds and tucks and ruffles and ribbons of his infantile grace—the insignia of his innocence, the vestiges of his heavenly creation — were to be ruthlessly rent away, and he was to make his *début* in the straight lines, plane surfaces, monotonous hues, and unmitigated bifurcations of the unbeautiful sex—the sex which is not lovely in itself, and which borrows no loveliness from its dress; for even the most thorough advocate of the equality of the sexes must admit that the handsome man is but a rough and primitive creation compared with the handsome woman, and that while the plain woman, by correct combinations of color and outline, can at least reduce her plainness to its lowest terms, and some-

times combine it altogether out of sight, the
plain man has nothing for it but to put on
his hat and coat and fight it out on that line.

Of course we all know that Harry must
come to it in time; but why array him pre-
maturely in the sombre garments of manhood? Why put his baby ignorance and innocence in such grotesque contrast with his
manly garb? It is only for his brief blossom-
ing that he can have the beauty of drapery.
Once out of it — he returns, he returns, he
returns no more. Once robbed of his cam-
brics and muslins, and there remains for him
through life nothing but a dreary waste of
trousers—a pitiless stretch of dun broadcloth,
scarcely brightened, certainly not relieved, by
the stiffness of starched and uncompromising
linen. The time may come in the flood-tide
of youth and love when he will put a bouquet
in his button-hole. In his famished craving
for color he may possibly indulge in a blue
necktie or a pink-bordered handkerchief; but

not for him the broad expanses of lustrous
hues; never for him the rainbow tints, the
sunset blendings, wherein his sister may lux-
uriate.   It is only the short, sweet morning
bloom of his babyhood that can be tricked out
in curve and color, in feathers and flowers and
all fantastic finery.

But the decree goes forth.   Off come the
bobbing little petticoats that I love, the plump
little sleeves so full of the plump little arms,
the baby waist that has nothing in common
with the tyrant man, and never so much as
suggests the arrogance and domination of the
oppressing sex—and Baby Harry goes into
breeches and ecstasies.

But I have my revenge.   With the robes he
has not put on the soul of manhood.   His awful innocence is too fresh from heaven to be
smothered by jacket and trousers.   He has by
no means yet unlearned the contortions and
climbings, the crawlings and rollings, of his
lost estate, and his clothes have hard work to

stay on. It is only by the skin of their teeth that the trousers keep connection with the jacket. He emerges from his dressing-room dainty and decorous, "close buttoned to the chin," collar straight, shoes tied, stockings fast —a little man. An hour passes, and the little man has one shoe off, the string of the other gone. One red stocking has been displaced by a black and white striped one, with the heel cocked defiantly over his instep, and the other stocking is reefed around his ankle. Both bare, brown, battered knees are surmounted with a white cotton crown, and the minute breeches are rucked up as high as they will go around the minute legs. Buttons have treacherously parted company with button-holes, and alow and aloft bears Harry his flags of truce. Dear little dilapidated man—comical little mockery and travesty of a man— manikin, midget, baby in breeches—such and so great confusion come upon all impatient and evil-minded parents who are not content to wait the flower's slow unfolding, but will have the tiny and tender bud spring suddenly into the broad-bannered rose!

"Harry Midget, come hither and be reconstructed. What did you see at the circus yesterday?"

" A leffalent an' a baby leffalent!"

" And where is Katrina gone?"

" Gone to Frank-an-cisco!"—pulling out for freedom.

"Stop! Tell me what is the Japanese embassador's name."

" I—*whack*-u-ra!"—tugging mightily away.

"How much do you love me? Then you shall go."

" *Tin*-dollar!"

" That all?"

" An' a gol' lockit!"

Bless the baby, with or without his "troublesome disguises," which, after all, rather emphasize than disguise his babyhood.

But when you come to the other baby, the

case is pitiful. To think of Baby Harry ab-
dicating in favor of this bit of scarcely an-
imated nature! Harry, all brightness and
quickness and sturdy strength, all determination and purpose, and eager liking and definite
will—and this little lump of flesh and flannel,
nothing but creases and folds and bulgings
and fumblings—and a girl at that!

But Harry the Magnanimous knows no en-
vyings nor jealousies. He cares not for crown
and throne, admires his little sister with whole-
souled enthusiasm, and shows her off to visitors as if she were a panorama and he the
exhibitor. "Dat's her hair," rubbing up the
golden haze that clouds her head. "See her
eyes!" and he pokes his dimpled fingers into
the staring, blinking orbs, under a firm conviction that it is an entire novelty for babies
to have eyes.

They are strange creatures, these babies.
You do not expect them to walk and talk, and
turn out their toes and be generally decorous;

but it does seem as if they might know enough
to keep their heads from dropping off their
shoulders. They do not. True, I never knew
a baby to jerk its head off, but no thanks to
baby. From honorable, even Christian motives, from a benevolent desire to evince your
sympathy with the fond parent, you hold out
your arms to receive the proffered infant. For
an instant all goes well, but the next, without
warning or provocation, down goes the head
back over your arm with a jerk, as if the ver-
tebræ were resolving themselves into their
original lime and phosphorus. And then a
baby is so voluminously dressed that you can
never be sure you have clutched the real article unless you take it by the neck, which
hardly agrees with baby, though it is the fa-
vorite mode of handling kittens. The trouble
is, there is nothing human about a baby. It
has no sympathy, no love, no hope nor fear.
It sometimes contorts its face into a grimace
which partial friends fondly call a smile, but

it is just as likely to be followed by a scream
as to subside into sobriety, and it certainly
looks as much like pain as pleasure. No, there
is no good in talking about it. The baby being here, and being subject to cold and heat
and hunger and thirst, must be warmed and
fed and sheltered; but as to being interesting—as to comparing it with Harry!

But the wonder, the marvel, the miracle!
Eastern jugglers show you a palm-tree bursting the soil, branching to the heavens, putting forth leaf and bud and fruit before your
eyes; but a baby is more wonderful than the
palm-tree. For the change has come, so
subtile that your eye can not see it. Even
while you were looking, even while you were
reviling the little atom, it ceased to be an atom,
and proved the truth of Professor Tyndall's
theory that an atom contains within itself the
promise and potency of every form of life.
Imperceptibly, undetected, the microcosm put
off its impersonality and stepped into the ranks

B

of humanity. The mite has found her soul.
In her eye is recognition, in her smile expression. How it came about none can tell: but
yesterday she was isolated, and to-day she is
linked with all the world. But yesterday she
was an interloper, and to-day she is a constitu-
ent part of the universe, with established and
acknowledged rights. Oh, but now she strikes
out gloriously into life, and puts her foes to
shame! No more aimless lopping heads for
her, but a stretching and setting in all directions whithersoever she would push her researches. Now for parents and nurses who
shall be humble and meek in spirit, and willing to follow nature, and not set up theories
founded on their own conceit! We shall never
cease to have the church broken up with dissensions between old school and new, the state
fuming over tariff and tax, families torn with
internal dissensions, until we bring up children logically. How can a man be logical
when his parents were continually interposing

to make him illogical from his infancy? A
child should be permitted to follow out his
own conclusions. The adult world agrees that
it is not polite to interrupt. The learned world
understands that the sequence of thought is
not to be lightly disturbed. Let us take our
politeness and our philosophy into the baby
world. The little sister is gazing steadfastly
at the chair. Her blue eyes are fixed and bulg-
ing. You will immediately begin to toss her
and coo to her, distract her attention, and pre-
vent her solution of the problem of the chair.
So her mind loses the power of fixation, and
by and by you will have an unreasonable and
unreasoning woman on your hands.

I, on the contrary, reverence her maiden
meditations, hold my peace, and simply and
silently watch her. Presently she stretches
out her tiny hand. Nature is fumbling for
the evidence of touch as well as sight. But
she can not quite reach the chair. She leans
forward. I obey nature and let her slip to-

ward the chair. She feels it all over with the
experimental hands. She applies to it her little toothless experimental mouth. Of course
she drools somewhat on the silk cover, but it
is far more important that a child should be
brought up logically than that a chair should
be kept unspotted. She evinces a desire to investigate the lower part of the chair and the
under part of the seat. Thoroughness, a disposition to go to the root of the matter, con-
tinuity of attention, are traits which can not
be too highly valued or too fully cultivated.
She leans out and strikes forward with a force
that shifts her centre of gravity. Nature, as
if for the very purpose of aiding her in the
pursuit of knowledge, has made her utterly
without fear. We adults should not dare to
look over a corresponding precipice; but she,
with blind faith in the unseen holding-back
power of the universe, flings herself forward.
I do not falsify her faith, but gather her long
petticoats, for such case made and provided,

into my hand, and, holding her like a bag,
let her descend head-first to look at the legs
and rungs of the chair. Prejudiced and self-
conceited adults make a great outcry, as if
you were letting the baby down to perdition :
but it is pure logic. I want her to continue
her investigations so long as they have interest for her. You talk about her brains.
Her brains are in her head, and turning her
upside down is not going to take them out.
Does not Nature know as much about her
brains as you and I, and would she impel her
downward, and keep her fumbling and stretching and staring, if it were not a good thing to
do ? Only be humble and not self-conceited,
and baby will presently give a sign that she is
through with that branch of the subject, and
ready to come right side up with care.

And up she comes, bright and satisfied, to
give the lie to all your narrow-brain theories,
and prepared to study the next subject with
the attention which befits a reasonable being.

And she has suddenly blossomed into beauty. There be who think she was always beautiful. "The baby is splendid!" said doting Partiality; while as yet no unprejudiced person could see aught but shapelessness and discoloration—a head sunk in shoulders, a pudgy, puffy wab. But the wab has unfolded like a flower. The stately head rises from the shapely shoulders, the yellow furze curls into silken hair. The nose asserts itself, the mouth unfolds and curves into Cupid's bow, the plump and perfect arm, the dimpled, dainty hand, rise and reach with matchless grace, or lie folded in tender repose. She looks and listens : what spirit in the erect head, in the straight and supple neck! what bold out-look in the eagle eyes! what brilliancy of tint, what purity of texture! It is a statue of breathing marble, but never was marble yet so fine and fair, nor is the inmost petal of the rose so soft. And all her whiteness is suffused with the bloom of life. She recognizes the voice that speaks, the

face that gazes, and her pose breaks into move-
ment. Leaps a sudden light into the eyes' unfathomable blue. The tiny rose-bud face is
shining all over with smiles. Legs and arms,
and the whole lithe little body, are astir and
aspring. It is the far-off hidden heart that
as yet has uttered no word of love, but feels in
its fastnesses the great throb of human sympathy, and darts out its swift and glad re-
sponse. Nay, more than that, the shy little,
sweet little, coy little woman — the Sleeping
Beauty that a score of years will scarcely
waken—breathes even now on the unconscious
air, and Baby turns quickly away from the too
fervid sunshine of your look, and buries her
happy face in nurse's sheltering shoulder.

The moral of both babies is this : we know
very little about it.

When I see the absolute ownership in and
control of their children which some parents
assume by virtue of their relationship, I marvel. The responsibility of a parent can not

perhaps be exaggerated. This little boy who
sits on the floor talking dreamily and dramat-
ically to himself as he plays with his blocks
may be warped and ruined by parental blun-
ders, may lose his life by parental neglect, or
the sound mind in the sound body may be
wisely guided to its greatest possibilities. But
no parental design can determine what those
possibilities shall be. It remains for observation to discover them. Herein lies the mistake of many: they will determine rather than
discover. They wish their boy to be a minister, like his fathers before him, and they shape
all his training to that end. But the boy does
not want to be a minister. He wants to be a
sailor. The blood of some old sea-king, dead
for generations, reddens anew in his veins, and
impels him irresistibly. Why it lay dormant
so long, what influences quickened it to life in
him, none can say. But the fact must be no-
ted and respected, or disaster will ensue. This
round-eyed baby, all dependent now on others,

is yet as distinct an individual as the emperor
on his throne. What traits he has selected
from his numerous ancestors doth not yet appear; but the selection is already made. The
parental part is wisely to cultivate what exists,
not ignore or repress it and cultivate what
the father wishes were there instead. The parental part is to stand in awe before that mysterious and fearful thing, a human being. In
youth, in maturity, in old age, it is still fearful;
but time has incrusted the soul, has developed
somewhat its powers, has given it expression
and self-direction, has made its features familiar to our eyes. The new soul comes fresh
from the unknown, itself all unknown. This
waxen-faced creature, with the rounded limbs,
the flaxen hair, the cooing voice, has been six
months in this rushing, tumultuous world, and
has never told us what she thinks of it. The
lips of him a thousand years dead are not
more securely sealed than hers.

When little Harry lay tossed and tortured

by cruel disease, whither fled in dismay his bright and eager mind? Where behind the dim and faded eyes lay the forces of thought and feeling? Locked in what evil spell lan guished the isolated soul? Torpid in heavy sleep through the early night, the midnight clock did not more surely strike than the de- mon of unrest came in upon him from the wide outer universe, and drove him through the slow, pitiless hours. What subtile sym- pathy linked this atom with the stars in their courses? What finest cosmic ether penetrates all space, and thrills both soul and substance? Is mind, then, only refined matter? Are we in very deed children of the clod?

"Mamma! mamma!" cries Harry, his great eyes clouded, his brow wrinkled with displeas- ure, his whole face set against outrage—"Mam- ma, *are* I sparkin' the girls? I want to go play with Bessie Mannin', and Ann say I sparkin' the girls!"

"Sparkin' the girls" is evidently some undesirable unknown quantity to this future man, whose boyhood is as yet only evolving itself from babyhood.   The baby in him goes about sucking the other baby's bottle with great delight, while the nascent boy is equally and simultaneously delighted to stride the yard-stick, which he picturesquely dubs his "straddle horse."   Nursing-bottle in one hand, equine yard-stick in the other, he walks along the parting of two ways, holding the winsome graces of both.   Not yet has fallen from him the awful innocence of infancy; but all his blood bounds with the strength and energy of masculine vigor.   When a new crying-doll is put into the tiny hands of the little sister, the boy-baby also goes moaning about for "a squeak-thing," and no nomenclature of his maturity could more happily hit off the clumsy directness of the male mind than this name he gives to the gutta-percha toy.

And the little lady who sits throned amid her pillows on the bed, and who, in spite of pillows, lunges now this way and now that in slow, vague, vain pursuit of the "squeak-thing" that is ever falling from her fumbling fingers —this little lady approves as unquestionably her right to belong to the oppressed sex. Small notice gets she from the other, though when she is actually thrust into a man's face, he will look up and say, "Ah! pretty little girlie!" and become immediately absorbed in his book. When, an hour after, she puts on some irresistible new attraction, and he is implored to "*look* at the little sister," he responds, abstractedly, "Yes, I did," as if he had given a note of hand to take account of stock in her once a day, and had kept his bond. For this stoical and monstrous indifference does the little girl show any resentment? Does she, as the very least of her duty, deny acquaintance with this unnatural parent, and stare or shriek her *spretæ injuria formæ?* Spiritless, abject, and servile specimen of her abject and servile sex! Born to be neglected and slighted, because she

permits slights! Not she! Whenever the
Grim Grendal enters the room this miserable
little damsel, doomed to be despoiled, pockets
all her slights, cranes her lovely neck, follows
the tyrant man with eager, delighted eyes, puts
forth all her witchery to wile him into notic-
ing her, and if my lord deign to hold out his
golden sceptre, all her face grows radiant with
smiles, and body and soul leap with ecstasy.
Silly little minx! to go into raptures over an
indifferent wooer! Stupid little Mädchen!
if only you would stand on your dignity, how
would you bring all the world to your feet!
More than now? Ah! that I know not!

> "Bright as the sun your eyes the gazers strike,
> And, like the sun, they shine on all alike."

But is it any harm to the sun that he shines
on all alike? Has he any the less light left
in his heaven of heavens? Is it not rather his
glory and unutterable joy that he shines and
shines out of his own heart, not heeding re-

turns, but flooding the wandering worlds with
warmth and beauty and color and life because
it is his nature and happiness to give?

Or does my little lady of the starry eyes
feel blindly somehow in her ignorant heart
that she was a fifth wheel in this coach, and
must justify her existence by rolling smoothly,
since there was no real need of her rolling at
all?   Truly she is wise in her generation, for
Malthus himself could not find it in his heart
to remand her to the blank eternities.   All she
asks is a little food, a little bed, and she flowers to the light, and folds at night the purest
lily that ever soared on slender stalk to greet
the gracious day.   Who shall grudge her the
joy of living, when she herself is a living joy?
But woe is me for the unhappy babies whose
life is a succession of wails!   Wrong — all
wrong.   Babies no more ought to cry than
grown people.   Yet you will hear it said of
such and such a baby that "the first three
months of its life it cried all the time," as if

you should say it had blue eyes. A baby cries because it is unhappy. The natural condition of life is happiness. They start out in life—when they start properly—with an immense surplus capital of contentment. A baby I wot of has been known to wear a needle sticking into her all day and never wince. I do not suppose she knew it was a needle. I suppose she thought it was the natural feeling to have when you are five months old. But, at any rate, she felt that life was too short and sweet to sacrifice serenity to a needle. So she smiled and smiled. Cry-babies indeed ! It is some ancestral sin or folly or ignorance that clouds the sunshine of life's morning hour.

But it is the little sister's evening hour. Soft as the petals of the apple blossoms, one by one fall the gossamer garments, till the baby sits clothed in her beauty, naked and unashamed. Oh, but then how she frisks and curvets and coos ! The caressing air, the boundless freedom, set all her nerves a-tingle.

Then how sweet to her seem her tiny toes, if only she could get at them! What vigorous dives she makes at hair and neckties and every thing within or without her reach! And presently, while she bounds and frolics, overflowing with the joy of life, we are aware that the window is darkened, and, lo! four little boy-faces pressing against the pane and gazing in with wide eyes of wonder and admiration at the minute morsel tossed aloft in a giant's stalwart arms.

And the minute morsel leaps and coos and crows and kicks with undisguised and undiminished exultation till cambric and sleep descend upon her, and all the darkened world curtains her repose.

II.

DEAD LEAVES.

THE " Lady-Bird " is a very charming periodical, published, edited, written, wholly, I suppose, by women, and is a creditable exhibition
of what women can do when they set about it.
But the charm of the Lady-Bird is not in the
tinkling ornaments about its feet, in its change-
able suits of apparel, and its mantles, and its
wimples, and its crisping-pins ; but in the fine
little feminine head that rises so stately, poised
with serene good sense, in the midst of a crooked and perverse generation.

The Lady-Bird sang a pleasant song one day
over the little ones rolling along the streets in
their fine little wagons, but it stopped not quite
soon enough for wisdom.   When its love-song
sank into the minor key of wailing, and it af-
firmed that " the childless must be aware that

C

they drop out of the world like dead leaves,
that they send no strength or vitality onward
to the future ; they have no bond with it, no
part in it, no right or room in the great and
perfect race which one day shall blossom out
of this; they fall by the way, and are no more"
—then the Lady-Bird spake as one of the foolish men speaketh, and I who love rebuke and
chasten.

Even botany weighed in the balance is found
wanting, which should be a solemn warning
never again to deviate from the path of rectitude.   The dead leaves, invoked, rise up from
their graves to bear swift witness against error.   "Dead leaves," they murmur, shivering,
shriveled on the apple-trees, massed in rustling
heaps under the maples, where the wild winds
have swept them—" dead, indeed, dead as Morley, dead as a door-nail now ; but have we indeed sent no strength or vitality onward to the
future ?   *Have* we no right nor part in the
great and perfect race of Baldwins and Astra-

khans and Gravensteins that lie in your bins,
to gather presently around your fireside and
minister at your family feasts? Dead leaves
as we are, we can tell you better than that.
Woman's paper as you are, you ought to know
better than that. The great and perfect race,
if it ever come, must come by our leading. It
is from us that the future gathered its strength
and vitality. Without us it would have been
deader than we are now; for it would have
been, like Morley, dead to begin with, whereas
we are only dead at the end. It is through us
that the fruit, the future, lives and breathes
and has its being.

And if you attempt to gainsay them, my
Lady - Bird, Wood and Grey will put you
down with a strong hand. The dead leaves
are right, and the living leaf is wrong.

Wrong, after the manner of men. It is
only when you forsake your own womanly
wisdom, and follow after false gods, that you
go astray. A paper that must be a great deal

wiser than you, because it is a man's paper,
and you are only a woman's paper; that must
be a great deal better than you, because it is a
religious paper, and you are only a worldly
paper; this great and good journal said, once
upon a time, speaking like you of the childless: " It is almost throwing away life, leaving
none to cheer you through life, comfort you in
old age, imitate and mourn you when dead . . .
leaving the world no larger or better, and no
influence to be handed down to the future."

Which is precisely your doctrine, dear Lady-
Bird; but do not yet exult.

In another column the same paper says:
" G. P. will sail for England about the first of
May, bearing with him the gratitude of a nation. He has caused his name to be ever remembered, and his benefactions have a scope
that will render them blessings to the end of
time."

But G. P. had never wife nor child, and his
benefactions consisted solely of money.

The self-same copy of the self-same paper
elsewhere announces that Miss S. S. has given
twenty thousand dollars to Andover Theological Seminary; and "who," inquires the paper,
in a gush of eloquent gratitude—"who can calculate its benign influence on the whole Christian Church and the world? Miss S. will by
this benefaction be doing good as long as time
shall last. Not only will thousands of holy
men, who in the lapse of time will receive
the education which this donation will furnish,
bless her name and keep fresh her memory;
but thousands of communities will be favored
with the refining and educating, the gladden-
ing and saving influences of the Gospel in
their midst, and thousands on thousands of
immortal souls will, we trust, be crowned with
the bliss of heaven as the fruit of it."

All that for twenty thousand dollars! What
more could a living leaf do?

In the same paper we are told that "a remarkable Christian has just fallen in death,

named E. R., a member of the Congregational Church in Arcadia. He was an independent farmer, plain and unassuming, but thoroughly consistent in his life, ready for every good work, and liberal in his pecuniary contributions for benevolent objects far beyond the ordinary standard. He had no children, and his wife was like-minded with himself. For several years they have given away *their whole income* beyond their necessary frugal support, the amount of their contributions being sometimes one thousand dollars per annum. He was seventy years of age at his death; and up to the day on which he was taken sick he worked industriously, and sought to acquire money as eagerly as any miser, but only for the purpose of bestowing it in charity. At his death he, by will, left all he had to his wife, with the proviso that what remained at her death should be devoted in equal proportions to the American Board, the American Home Missionary Society, the American Mis-

sionary Association, and the education of
young men for the ministry. . . . The societies
will probably realize several thousand dollars
each. His case illustrates strikingly the great
amount of good a plain and unostentatious,
though earnest and consistent Christian can
do. His influence was mighty."

All Lady-Birds can see how unsafe it is to
teach for doctrine the commandments of men.
One can never tell where is the end of that
hunting. If one will follow this creed, he
must add another clause. He who would bind
himself to the future must do it through his
children; or, add the Tetzels who have not
yet met their Luther, he must give a certain
sum of money—twenty thousand dollars at the
close of life will suffice; whether a less sum
would answer, or whether discount would be
offered at an earlier period, does not appear—
to a theological seminary; or, if he can not
give twenty thousand in a lump, he may com-
pound on his whole income for a series of

years—except his necessary frugal expenses.
Mark, they must be frugal. Thus says religion.
Why should the world be more strenuous?

A young woman was brought up with a
brother, between whom and herself existed
a peculiar and profound attachment. She
kept house for him until he was married; but
then, finding her occupation gone, she became
restless and uneasy. He observed it, inquired
the cause, and asked her what sort of life she
really would like. She replied that she would
like to have a large house under her own control, and to gather into it as many outcast or
neglected children as it would hold, and take
care of them. He came home at night, told
her the house was ready, and that she might
collect her vagabonds as soon as she chose.
She was as good as her word. She went out
into the highways and hedges, and brought in
the little wretches. Family after family she
gathered around her; and many, perhaps scores,
of children were rescued by her from degra-

dation and crime, and reared to happiness and honor.

Who will say that that woman sent no strength or vitality onward to the future, and had no part nor right nor room in it?

The very essence of motherhood was there, the spirit and soul of all womanly character. It is impossible accurately to compute the results of moral causes, yet, so far as it is possible to judge, that woman sent more vitality into the future, had a stronger hold upon it and a greater right in it, than half a dozen selfish or shallow mothers. That the children were not her own only strengthens her claim upon the gratitude of the great and perfect race which is to come. The mother simply discharges a duty which she creates. She does that which she would be inhuman, a monster, not to do. This woman took upon herself the work which of right belonged to others. She burdened herself with evils for which she was not even remotely responsible.

She doubly aided the state; not simply by adding to its number of virtuous and intelligent citizens, but by creating virtue and intelligence out of crime and ignorance. That which was fatal disease she converted into vital force. Out of the strong she brought forth sweetness.

Will any one dare to stand up and affirm that she will drop out of the world like a dead leaf, that she will send no strength nor vitality onward to the future, and has no right nor room in it?

The world has heard of Mary Lyon. We know with what earnestness, with what enthu siasm, with what fidelity she devoted her whole life to the education of other people's children. She made her living by it indeed; but such was the zeal, such the fervor which she threw into her work, that it seemed not so much a profession as a consecration. She was only one of a class who, with less enthusiasm, perhaps, but with equal fidelity, occupy them-

selves with the training of the young. They
have often no children of their own; but the
influence which they exercise upon the children of others—it is, perhaps, not too much
to say—is unbounded. It is certainly incal-
culable. It carries forward the work begun
in good homes; and in thousands of cases it
helps to counteract the evils and to supply the
deficiences of bad ones. There are men and
women the world over who trace back to wise
and competent teachers those formative principles which have moulded their lives to symmetry and success.

And we gaze at them open-eyed, and assure
them that those teachers sent no strength nor
vitality onward to the future, and have no
right to any share in its excellence.

Or, to look at it in another light, is it
through their children that parents always get
their strongest hold upon the future? Is it
Milton's poetry and essays or Milton's daughters that have borne his strength onward to

our own time? Is it Shakespeare's plays or
Shakespeare's Susanna that gives him his place
in the world of to-day? Is it Madame D'Arblay's book or Madame D'Arblay's boy, is it
Scott's novels or Sir Walter's heir that constitutes the bond between the past and the
present? George Washington and St. Paul
dropped out of the world like dead leaves, and
the glory of a man is not in the grandeur of
his life, the wholesomeness of his example, but
in the fact that he leaves a family of children!

O Lady-Bird, you are a hypocrite; and
they that say the same are like unto you;
and so is every one that trusteth in you. You
know quite well that what you honor is in-
tegrity, purity, humanity, reverence, unselfish-
ness. He who meets the duties of life, who is
honorable, high-minded, public-spirited, who is
considerate, careful, kind at home, faithful,
charitable, comprehensive abroad, loyal and upright every where—he is the man who serves
his country best, and deserves well of the fut-

ure, whether his children praise him in the gates, or whether, like one we wot of, God make him childless that a nation may call him Father.

The leaf that is green and fresh and shapely, that breathes in life for the bud and furthers the perfect tree—that is a living leaf, and in its royal present enfolds the royal future. It has no quarrel with the rounded and ripening fruit, but lends itself with ardor to the development of the life from which both sprang, and to whose continuance and symmetry both must perforce give help or hinderance. But when some amateur orchardist goes by, and would approve his wisdom by speaking evil of its dignity, it may, perhaps, be pardoned for glancing somewhat disdainfully around upon the knobby, knurly fruit, the many sour, dwarfed, misshapen, worm-eaten apples, and querying whether his science may not be better applied to improving the quality of the crop than decrying the mission of the leaf.

The leaf's death is in accord with its life. It dies because its work is done—its vital and divine work. It has softened the splendor of blossom and sheltered and nourished the growing fruit. Its service is over; for a little season it flames into a brilliancy all its own, and then floats gently down to rest and resurrection. Never was man or woman born who might not be glad to drop out of the world as drops the dead leaf—its mission perfectly accomplished, its influence never to be defined.

And though we, or an angel from heaven, preach any other gospel unto you, let him be accursed.

Yet another gospel is so strenuously preached that we should not be surprised if its echoes penetrate where truer notes are expected. There are prophets of a new dispensation who teach that the strength of a nation as of a family consists not in quality but in quantity.

Whenever there is a lull of the elements; whenever war, famine, fraud, freshet, drought, pestilence, explosion, collision, and tempest subside enough to leave us a brief repose, some medical, clerical, or otherwise statistical marplot is sure to appear on the scene and spoil our peace by affirming that the native American is passing away. It is not enough that we are breaking our hearts over his death by field and flood, but we must break them into still smaller fragments over the fact that he is not born. There are persons who hold this in reserve when all other sorrows fail them; and there are patriots whose whole stock in trade consists of vital statistics, and the bewailings thereunto appertaining. Their literary preparation seems to be in walking about the streets counting the children; and when they have ascertained that the large families are of Irish descent, and that the native Americans average only three and a half to a family, they are happy. Then is our American race swiftly dismissed to annihilation; then is our continent incontinently deluged

with Irish blood; then is the Bible brandished over us like a scourge of small cords; then
cometh our fear as desolation, and our de-
struction as a whirlwind.

"The Bible every where," says one of these
Cassandrian prophets, "holds up the thought
that a great family is a special blessing." If
special, perhaps it is idle to expect that it
should be general; but if our vital statistician
would take his horse and chaise, and drive
around to the great families of the Bible, he
would have reason to blow his melancholy
blast as long and loud among the hills of Ju-
dea as in the valleys of New England. The
laws and customs of marriage among the Jews,
considered from our point of sight, were de-
graded and disgusting. It was not dishonor-
able for a man to transfer his daughter to a
husband without regard to her wishes or feelings. A man might have as many wives as he
chose; and any or all of them he could dis-
card at will, with no restraint except that he

should give to the discarded wife a certificate
of the fact, a bill of divorcement—a liberty
prized so highly down even to the time of
Christ that, when he would enforce the perma-
nence of the marriage relation, men revolted
against marriage. They would not be married
at all if they must be married so strenuously!
"If the case of the man be so with his wife, it
is not good to marry." What characters are
nurtured under such laws and in such society
may easily be inferred; and may, indeed, be
read any where in the Old Testament. Doubtless the Mosaic code was exactly and admira-
bly adapted to the education of the Jew, as he
existed when that code was promulgated; but
to hold up the laws given to him as the rule
of our faith and practice, to hold up the ambi-
tions and aspirations of women reared under
such a dispensation as a model for our American
can women, is a measure not likely to increase
our respect for the vital statistician.

But even his count is questionable. Three

D

and a half children to a family is the burden
of his lamentations. The American mother
"leading round a solitary, lonely child" is his
bête noir. Yet, after all, this degenerate American mother is not a black swan among the
races. I am not sure that even the Hebrew
mother would bear away the palm from her.
Eve began the peopling of the world with an
indefinite number of sons and daughters; but
she was nearly a hundred and thirty years old
before her third child was born, and if she
lived in the present generation of Americans,
she would fall far below the average admitted
by our weeping philosopher. Sarah is the next
woman of whom we have any minute account,
and her Heraclitus would have seen doing
what he particularly stigmatizes — "leading
round a solitary, lonely child;" and he would
have had to wait ninety years to see her do
even so much as that. Rebekah and Rachel
would mount but a step higher in his estima-
tion, being each the mother of only two chil-

dren. Jacob's family does, indeed, figure largely in the sacred records; but the twelve sons
and one daughter, divided among the four
women who were their mothers, gives only an
average of three and one fourth to each, while
the admitted average of New England families is three and a fraction. Adah was the
mother of one child, Aholibamah of three,
Bashemath of one, Asenath of two, Jochebed
of three, Zipporah of two, Naomi of two, Elish-
eba of four. There seems to be no record of
Deborah's children. Probably she had none,
and if she had they were of no account. All
we know of her husband he owes to his wife.
Ruth had one child, Hannah six. Michal, we
are expressly told, had no child unto the day
of her death. Considering the small number
of women whose names and histories are re-
corded in the Bible, the testimony is over-
whelmingly in favor of small families. It
must be admitted either that they represent
the race, and that the Hebrew mothers gener-

ally had small families; or, if they do not represent the race, that the most prominent, distinguished, and advanced women among the
Hebrews had but few if any children. The
women here called to account average only
two and a small fraction, to the three and a
larger fraction of the New England mothers.
The effect of concentrating the ability, the affection, and the care of the mother on two
children, rather than dispersing it over a large
number, seems to have been most happy. The
Jewish race is so signally as to be considered
even miraculously endowed with vitality. Its
imperishable vigor is seen in the fact that
scarcely any art or science, any form of skill
or sagacity or enterprise, but has had, and I
might almost say has to-day, a Jew at its head.
Even the masses of the Jews have ever wrest-
ed prosperity from adversity, and lived in the
forefront of death.

To sum up the whole matter, we should say
that the Bible teaches that among the Hebrew

women children were a "special blessing,"
few in number, eagerly and passionately desired. As a result, we have a race of insur-
mountable strength, existing, increasing, flour-
ishing in the face of every obstacle. Our ancestors, according to the vital statistician, had
large families—twice and thrice and four times
as large as the Jewish mothers; and, as a result, we are already, in the second and third
generations, rapidly dwindling and deteriorating.

So, then, the vital statistician is not wrong
in blowing his warning blast; only he ought
to reverse his trumpet, and blow according to
the law and the testimony, until the average
American family is reduced to the Scriptural
standard.

The sufferings of the census-takers it is not
necessary to attempt to assuage. There is a
large class, not quite discontented, yet not
wholly content, to whom one would gladly
administer tranquillity. The great number of

women, old and young, who send articles to
the newspapers and magazines, is rather a
theme for badinage and slightly contemptuous
comment; yet it has its pathetic side. Some
are but fanciful and ambitious girls, who have
just left school, and wish to win fame. Some
simply have no especial ability for any occupation, and are attracted by the results of suc-
cessful writing. Others, unhappy, turn to literature because they must do something and
can do nothing. Others wish to lighten the
sorrows of the world and to do good. Many
have apparently a real ability, but family cares
interpose. The girl's early aspirations never
die, and once in a while some story or poem
breaks forth so good as to make her a little
dissatisfied that she can do no more and no
better. These latter women are clever, of active mind, of quick perception, of ready wit,
who could do well a great many things, but
who are confined to the one occupation of domestic life. The drudgery and routine weary

them. They long to escape to calm regions,
to nervous tranquillity and mental exhilara-
tion. They are appreciative readers, intelligent mothers, capable women; but they are
not without an occasional pang at the thought
of what they might have accomplished in other ways and walks.

I shall not be suspected of exalting the domestic above every other career. There are
those who have no vocation for what is com-
monly understood as the family life. The
commonplace routine of housekeeping over-
powers, for them, its pleasant possibilities.
There are, besides these, a great host of women
who, whatever may be their tastes and capa-
bilities, yet feel it best to remain outside the
family circle. To all such, business, art, literature, lie open. They are unembarrassed, free
to follow any career. They should not only
be countenanced, but encouraged. Independence, ease, fame, honor, are all within their
grasp, and are the lawful guerdon of their

struggle. Nothing less than the highest should be their aim, and no sacrifice should be counted too great in its pursuit.

But I wish I could persuade the women who are enlisted in another army, that they, too, fight under no contemptible flag. It is not simply that the mothers of busy, growing families have not time to take the necessary steps for becoming famous. Even had they the time, the chances are very much against their success. If a man or woman, impelled by genius, write an immortal poem, that is the world's gain. But if you calculate chances, they are just as many that a woman will acquire fame through her children as through her writings. It is true that, having devoted all her energies to bringing up her family, it will be found in the end that they are but respectable, commonplace men and women. But also, if she had written a book, it would very likely have been but a respectable, commonplace book—a book no more remarkable among books than her man among men.

No woman should think of being a writer
unless she is willing and able to give her life
to it; to give, let us say, for definiteness, as
much time, money, devotion, as the clergyman,
the doctor, the lawyer gives to preparation for
his profession. A woman may write a poem
for her own pleasure, may send a letter to a
newspaper, just as she may mix a medicine or
preach to her Sunday-school class. But before
she asks opinion as to whether she have sufficient mental power to be a writer, let her ask
herself whether she have sufficient circumstan-
tial freedom. It is the old theological question of moral and natural ability. Literature
is fascinating, and its perquisites delightful;
but it is also exacting, imperious, inexorable.
The writer is stimulated by recognition, but he
does not beforehand weigh his work in the
scale with recognition. If he think of fame
and money and doing good, he is moved from
without, not from within. He is thinking of
the recompense; he is not inspired with his

work. He is thinking of what is to come from
the world to him, not fashioning what is to go
out from himself to the world. The true
writer thinks of none of these things. He
simply writes. Somewhat in him craves expression. He does not balance probabilities.
He does not stipulate for certainties. He is
troubled by no fears of friendly disappointment. He does not consult friends. Whoever
reasons, is lost. The world is so full of good
writing that the argument is wholly against
writing any more. But instinct, the inward
prompting, is stronger than reason. The writer
born thinks of nothing outside, but is impelled
from within. He broods in secret. He con-
ceals his work. He averts suspicion. He does
not resolve to study. He studies because he
craves knowledge as the flower craves light.
His writing is like that flower's unfolding. It
is a result, not a means. It is a development,
not a determination. He never questioned
what he should make of himself; but before

consciousness dawned upon him or ever the
world was aware, suddenly his thought, his
dream, his fancy burst into blossom. Then
fame found him, and money flowed in upon
him, and friends rejoiced over him. But of
all bud and bloom and fruitage, its seed is in
itself.

Suppose, now, the clever but full-handed
house-mother might become an interesting
writer, how shall she set about it? She is,
by her own confession, so absorbed in family
cares that she has no more leisure time than
she needs for her own recreation. These family cares she does not propose—as it is doubtless impossible for her—to relinquish. Her
literary acquisitions and practice must come,
in addition to duties which already fully occupy her life. Would not one say that the
burden was too great; that the attempt to
conquer two different and difficult kingdoms
would endanger health, peace, and happiness;
and that, after all, she would have written

nothing better than already exists, even in our accessible English literature?

Why not choose an easier path? Suppose that, when her daily tasks are over, she turn to reading, instead of writing. Her weary mind is stimulated, but not spurred. She is brought at once into close and confidential communication with the world's best intellects. She is furnished with information. She is lifted above the plane of every-day life. Imagination and taste are cultivated; and, for the exercise of her formative power, she has always her family and her friends. The fancies, dreams, theories, convictions, to which she would gladly give voice through her pen, may find voice through her lips. Writing a book, painting a picture, bringing up a child, are only different ways of doing the same thing. In all of them we are influencing mind, shaping character. There be shallow philosophers, superficial observers, who would have the world believe that women are womanly only when

they are literally taking care of children. Let
us not therefore fall into the opposite error of
supposing that they can rise to their loftiest
intellectual heights only by writing. There is
a great deal of mechanical in literary work.
There is a great deal of mental in domestic
work. The best writers do not depend solely
upon the fires of heaven to forge their metal,
but hammer and chisel and polish like any
blacksmith. The finest mother looks not after
mush and milk and shoes and stockings alone,
but takes all knowledge to be her province,
and makes her children princes and princesses
therein. Just as we would counsel the woman who has chosen art, science, or literature,
never to vex herself because she can not combine with it the intricate home career; so
would we counsel those who have chosen the
home, not to be disturbed because the toils and
rewards of other lives are not theirs. We can
not all do every thing. Theirs is certainly not
the least honorable, the least absorbing, nor

the least satisfactory choice; and having made it, they should not only be content, but eager to make all things subordinate to it. She who writes a book, touches many minds. She who rears a child, moulds one. But the many minds are only touched; the one mind is moulded. The influence which the two women exert may be equal in quantity and dignity. They are different only in the forms of administration. The author diffuses; the mother concentrates. The book and the baby preach one gospel— that the only work of vital and lasting importance is the fashioning of human character. In the court of last resort, all work is worthy or worthless according as it bears on the welfare of the race; and in this work the mother may find scope for every faculty, and gratification for all pride.

III.

BRINGING UP PARENTS.

As between children and grown people, it is the grown people that need training.

When Archie began to go to school he was a good boy. He had his teasings and his tempers; but his conscience was alert, his sensibility acute, his delicacy unimpaired. The slightest touch of ridicule, or even .an unexpected notice of him, would stain his tiny cheek with an exquisite blush. So he went to school, the little virgin soul, full of keen expectation. What next? Why next Archie was getting discredits; Archie was having his ears pulled and boxed; Archie was being shaken and pinched and punished in small ways till he had ceased to care for it. He was not merely indifferent to the pain, which was trifling, but he had lost his sense of the shame of it, which was only not murder. Now I maintain that all the sin which Archie ever committed since he was born was not equal to his teacher's sin in thus rudely and ruthlessly brushing the bloom from his little heart. If any one were to be pinched and pulled and shaken, it was she, not he. Archie was taken away, before virtue was quite gone out of him, and sent to another teacher. Here his wasted gardens began to put forth blossoms again. One day the children ran in to the teacher, crying that Archie had said a wicked word. "No," she said, "I think not. Archie is a good boy." But after school she took him on her lap, and shone upon him till the little flower-soul softly opened itself and revealed that he had "said it was a damn hot day, but he heard a boy in Chestnut Street say it;" and in the same virtue by which he learned his letters he spoke his wicked word. So he was soothed and taught and dismissed, and not demoralized.

Children, according to my observation, are usually good, except so far as they are tampered with by their elders. They come into the world without any fixed bad habits, and we immediately turn to and fasten our own bad habits upon them, and call it family government. And pretty work we make of it. Family government is a good thing, but it ought to be exercised largely on the fathers and mothers. Conscientious parents grow serious over the weight of responsibility resting upon them, lament their ignorance of the best way to bring up children, and talk much of rules and system. But the best system in the world for children is to let them alone. The most rational, as well as the most righteous, resolve a parent can make over the new-born soul is the resolve of Moses at the burning bush: "I will now turn aside and see this great sight." On the contrary, he seems too often rather to pursue Nebuchadnezzar's line of reflection: Is not this great Babylon that

E

I have built? Is not this little Baby that *I*
have created by the might of my power and
for the honor of my majesty? No, it is not.
Every child is the child of man as truly as if
there were no God, but he is also the child of
God as truly as if there were no man. Behold,
all souls are mine : as the soul of the father, so
also the soul of the son is mine, saith the Lord.
You have taken the responsibility of summon-
ing him to life, and you therefore owe him
every thing which he needs. By your duty
and your love to him he is yours, and by no
other bond. He belongs to himself. He is an
independent being. His life is no more to be
bent to your ends, his tastes and talents are no
more to be moulded to the honor of your majesty, than if he were born on another planet.
You have absolutely no right over him, except
such as is created by your obligation toward
him. What that is can be determined not by
preconceived system, but by close and loving
observation of each individual case.

The only organic difference between children and grown-up people is that children are not grown up. Yet we often act as if they were another order of being, not amenable to the same laws as ourselves. On the contrary, they are precisely like us. They are open to reason just as we are, only rather more so. What is best for us is best for them. If we like to be treated with kindness, consideration, courtesy, so do children. If children ought to be polite to parents, parents ought to be polite to children.

One day a lady called who was very fond of Bertie: so Bertie was brought in. He was just ready to go out to play, with coat and mittens on, and comforter well tied down over his cap; so I said, "I think Mrs. S—— will excuse you, Bertie, for keeping your cap on a few minutes." Bertie went through his part promptly and properly enough, and I dismissed him to his sled; but he lingered; then I said, "If you choose to stay, Bertie, I will take your

cap off for you." But from some cause or
other Bertie chose neither to go nor to have
his cap off; and the upshot was, I marched the
little boy out of the room in disgrace. I was
not angry—I was surprised, and it seemed the
only thing to do; yet somehow I wish I had
not done it. The very fact that it did surprise
me, that it was not like Bertie, should have
held me back. When a man of good reputation does something which contradicts his past
life, we suspend judgment. We give him the
benefit, then, of his fair fame. Bertie's good
name should have shielded him from swift
judgment. Again, it is not considered good
taste for grown people to quarrel when company is present. If the husband is ill-humored
and grouty before guests, the wife turns it
skillfully aside with graceful pleasantry, and
makes the rough places plain. When she is
alone with him, if she is a good wife, mindful
of her marriage vows, she gives him a sound
moral drubbing; but before company she will

make every thing go smoothly or die. I should
have done the same with Bertie. What right
had I to mortify him and embarrass my guest
by giving prominence to his momentary ill-
manners? At heart I do not think he was ill-
mannered. Probably the chief cause of his
misbehavior was shyness, for shyness expresses
itself in many strange ways. If I had taken
no notice of Bertie's behavior at the time, but
had afterward showed him its impropriety, and
perhaps told him that when I had another visitor I should not be able to let him enter the
room, I think I should have done all the good,
and missed all the harm that the other course
wrought. To be sure, the visitor would have
thought that Bertie was not very well brought
up; but which is most important, that Mrs.
S —— should think Bertie is brought up well,
or that Bertie should be brought up well? But
there is no High Court of Appeal for children,
so Bertie was sent to Coventry all the after-
noon; and at supper we Pharisees gathered

high and mighty around the table, while the poor little publican and sinner sat in his rocking-chair by the fire, eating the bread and butter of bitterness, and making pathetic little well-bred attempts to ease off the situation by entering into talk as if nothing had happened; in all of which he was persistently snubbed, and, finally, had to ask my pardon. Oh! Bertie, little abused apostle of goodness, I ask *your* pardon! Will a thousand kisses make it up? Will a cunning little hem-stitched handkerchief, and two pairs of stockings all striped up and down, and the brightest of little scarlet gloves, and a ton of candy, be any atonement?

The very best method to bring up a child in the way he should go is to go in that way yourself. Be yourself that which you wish your child to be. If parents would " behave themselves," family government might speedily become one of the lost arts. Let the father and mother be civil, considerate, patient, sweet-tempered, low-voiced, obliging, truthful, and ten-

der, and pretty much all they would need do
to their children would be to stand aside and
see them grow! A child's heart, immeasur-
ably dear and close as it is, is also and forever
distinct and inscrutable. One can not always
see into it to straighten out the kinks, but one
can look into his own heart and control that;
and, seeing your wise and beneficent self-control, your child insensibly learns to govern his
own little waywardnesses, and becomes good
without knowing it. The ill-behavior of children is the direct and logical consequence of
the ill-behavior of their parents. The fathers
eat sour grapes in plain sight, and the children's teeth can hardly help being set on edge.
The parents behave like children, and then expect their children to behave like mature persons. The mother maltreats her child into
fretfulness and disobedience, and then shuts
him up in a closet for punishment, when she
ought to shut herself in the closet with ashes
on her head. The only mitigating considera-

tion is that the parents are themselves the victims of *their* parents' errors, and so we get back, by short and easy stages, to Adam and original sin.

On the other hand, we rarely see a well-behaved family of children where there seems to be any thing in particular going on to make them so. They seem to come up like a flower of their own sweet nature. They move easily among themselves, like the atoms of a drop of water, yet, like those atoms, make a symmetrical whole. There is neither rule nor misrule; in fact, there is not much government. Every thing goes without saying. There is no system except to follow nature; and nature prescribes, for children as well as for adults, for individuals as well as for nations— freedom. If a child abuse that freedom, let him be punished as nature punishes — by the consequences of his act, not by an arbitrary infliction. For instance, we say, truly, that obedience is very desirable, and may be

taught to a year-old child. A spoon lies on
the table, and the mother forbids the baby in
her lap to touch it. By a series of stern looks
and approving looks, and perhaps a smart pat
or two, and some crying on Baby's part, the
lesson is taught, and Baby henceforth knows
better than to touch the spoon. Then we all
turn up our eyes and say how judicious is that
mother, and how well - reared that family !
But, really, is any thing gained ? To be sure
the child has learned to obey his mother, but
he has learned it arbitrarily; and a good end
is not necessarily reached when one human
being has simply learned to submit his will to
a stronger will or a stronger force. What the
world needs is not weaker wills, but wiser wills
—wills under the control of reason and righteousness. Put such things as are destructible
beyond Baby's reach, and then let him make
all the investigations he pleases. Is the land
groaning under its weight of awakened mind
that we should build barricades around awak-

ing mind? The child will begin to be stupid and passive full soon enough. After a certain period the mind seems to double-lock all its gates, and forbid entrance to any more ideas; but while it is inquisitive let us help and not hinder it. A child is a philosopher pursuing his researches. He takes as much delight in a table full of dishes as the natural historian does in a river full of fishes. Will he break them if allowed to handle them? So does the man kill the fishes. But we do not, on that account, tie his hands behind him; on the contrary, we send him up the Amazon to fish all he will, and call it science. Nature shows us just how to manage it, if we only would look and listen. She makes the baby so small and weak that he can not get at any thing which he can hurt. He has to fumble all over his little face with his little fist, trying to rub his little nose, and then he does it in a back-handed, uncertain fashion. It is a long leap toward manhood when he can get his

dear little toes into his dear little mouth. Nature keeps him so small that he can not reach
things till he is capable of handling them. It
is we who balk nature, and wreak it on the
baby. We drop the table-cloth down straight
into the baby's hands, and then are vexed because he pulls it off. "Good Heavens, Mad
am!" a reasonable baby might say, "why was
that thing hanging down here if not for me to
clutch it? What were my hands given me for
but to use? Chain up your coffee-pot, and
don't tumble it down on my head!"

Must children, then, be suffered to have their
own way in every thing?

Generally, yes. Why not? Grown people
have their way. If the parents are good and
wise, the children will naturally take the right
way. If the parents are not good and wise,
the children's way will probably be nearer
right than the parents'. The chubby hand
throws down the spoon in a pet. You can
pick it up and smite the wayward hand. But

the more excellent, because the more natural, course is to take no notice of it, and let the spoon lie there. Nature teaches men and women by showing them and making them bear the result of their actions. She would teach children the same way if we did not interfere. Baby cries over his lost spoon; but let him cry. Crying is natural and wholesome, and, ten to one, far more sensible than the talk which it supplants. Who, for the mere sound of the thing, would not rather hear a baby cry all day than to hear most men—and women, too, for that matter — talk about woman's sphere? When the baby cries, he does his best; but when his aged relatives talk, you feel that they have not dealt fairly by the sense which their Creator originally gave them.

The mistake is in supposing that a child's "own way" is the wrong way. It is we old people whose ways are wrong. We will not take the trouble to be calm, unselfish, generous, self-controlled ourselves, but we pay to

those virtues the tribute of imposing them on
our children. "Now, Neddy, be generous,"
says papa, "and give little brother half your
plums." And if Neddy do it not, a ton of
Sunday-school literature is ready to bury him
alive with horror. Very well. Now, when
Neddy's papa's uncle dies, and leaves Neddy's
papa ten thousand dollars, let us see him turn
about and give *his* brother half of that plum!
"It is very wrong for Katy to quarrel with
her little sister." And then Katy is treated to
a long and serious talk, which makes her feel
very miserable and wicked till she has sobbed
out her sorrow, and kissed her little sister, and
offered up in atonement every valued possession she has in the world. And then Katy's
papa goes down to his office and writes an ed-
itorial which nips his neighbor's newspaper in
every other line, and never a sob sobs he over
his sin ; but if you upbraid him, he stands up
for it and laughs at you, and says all is fair in
love and war. Bringing up children, indeed!

If you want pure, unadulterated virtue, go to
the children.   Find me among the annals of
any extant Christian Church a finer example
of perfect self-sacrifice, of smiling, unconscious
heroism, of sweet, instantaneous adaptation to
the frailty of the weaker vessel, than was displayed by James the Greatest, saint and martyr, when his mother—hurried, worried, and
wearied—called him in from his play to be
dressed, and brandished the comb through his
hair not too gently: "That's right, mamma!"
cried Jamie.   "Yank it all you want to!"

A little boy was investigating the waiting-
room of a railroad station.   He was perhaps
five years old, with a flushed face, very dusty
and dirty; but his clothes were good, and he
might have been clean in the morning.   He
seemed quietly amusing himself, when a rough
voice said, "Look here! do you want me to take
you out-doors and give you a good whipping?
Well, I will if you don't behave.   Come here
and sit down.   Now sit still."   The speaker

was a tall young fellow, looking not more than
twenty years old, accompanying a woman who
might have been his mother or his wife; and
neither of them had sense or affection enough
to let the child run about the room, disturbing
no one, but insisted on his sitting still between
them. Of course the little fellow screamed,
and the big fellow jerked him down all the
harder, and threatened to whip him, and to put
him out of the window, and made ten times as
much trouble as the child would have made if
let alone. In fact, so far as appeared, the
right was, as usual, wholly on the child's part,
who was but following a nature which had
had only four or five years to be spoiled in,
while the man had been spoiling for twenty
years. Now there is no tyranny more absolute than the tyranny of an adult over a child.
Power, position, every thing is on his side;
and on the child's side utter moral, mental,
and spiritual helplessness. Such power in the
hands of a low, stupid, cruel nature is some-

thing appalling. I can not think of any remedy, except, perhaps, a punishment which shall be homœopathic in quality and allopathic in quantity. For instance, it would be excellent for a strong man to come along with a horsewhip and make this young fellow stand on his head, and whenever he flags a little, swaying to this side or that, give him a smart cut, or a dozen cuts, with the whip. It is just as reasonable to demand Twenty Years to stand on his head three quarters of an hour, as to require Four Years to sit still three quarters of an hour. And possibly the position might force a little sense into his skull. In its normal attitude it certainly held none.

It is a great mistake to keep children too long or too entirely in a state of pupilage. Few things so dwarf a child's mind and irritate its temper as the constant and necessarily petty exercise of authority. A child should be thrown on its own responsibility just as fast and just as far as possible. The needless in-

tervention of adults, even though made in and
with the tenderest kindness, is injurious to both
intellectual and moral character. Better a
child should have many tumbles, and walk
alone, than be upheld always by his mother's
hand. Children would learn to reason far
more than they do if their elders were not so
eager to reason for them. And if children
were more accustomed to use their reason,
there would not be so much false assumption
and insufficient induction among grown people. Let things follow each other naturally,
and the little folks will very soon be logical
without knowing it.

Jenny's heart is set on wearing her new silk
dress to the picnic. Her mother thinks it is
not a fit dress, and refuses—and does it all for
Jenny's good, the martyr — and Jenny cries
and pouts and sulks, and is very unhappy, and
shall be glad when she grows up and can wear
her best clothes at her liking.

How would it do, now, for Jenny's mamma

F

to let her wear the silk dress ?   She tells Jenny that it is not in good taste ; that she must be so careful not to soil and spoil it that she can not enjoy the picnic; that, whether this is spoiled or not, she can not have another silk dress to take its place; but she shall decide for herself.   I believe, ten to one, Jenny would agree with her mother, and be charming in her white piqué.   But suppose she yields to the sheen of the silk.   She goes to the picnic party, takes great thought for her raiment the first half-hour, and then—if she is a nice little girl — forgets all about it, sails in the boat, and splashes her dress ; eats ice-cream, which trickles on the flounces ; drops her sandwich in her lap buttered side down, and comes home altogether a sore spotted, and dilapidated little maiden.   Then the unnatural mother need not stand up with an I-am-holier-than-thou air, and add to the midget's distress by saying, " I told you so."   She may comfort and calm her, and assure her that life is tolerable even after one has spotted one's only silk gown. But there is the spotted dress teaching Jenny the inexorableness of law, the necessity of prudence, the wisdom of parents. It has no tenderness, no affection for Jenny, and all her sighing will not minish aught of stain or splash. Every time Jenny puts it on the ugly defacements say to her, "Jenny, your mamma was right. It is better to wear wash goods to picnics, in order that you may not have to wear shabby silks a year afterward." So Jenny learns to respect her mother's authority, and to judge of fitness in garments, and has thus started on the way of prudent, careful womanhood.

No; she does no such thing, because her fond and tidy mother steps in and spoils every thing. What! let her child wear that shabby dress to dancing-school and church? Let those stains and spots stay on? She would be considered a tidy housekeeper, indeed—a thrifty woman, a careful mother! Not she!

So she upsets all the arrangements of Providence, takes out the grease with French chalk and warm iron, puts in a new breadth for the splashed one, and sends Jenny forth, smiling and happy and fresh as new, and therefore not in the least benefited by her experience. Because her mother has interposed between error and its result, Jenny will forget both. Mamma acts for Jenny's good, does she? Oh no! it is for the good of Jenny's gown; it is for the good of her own name. She forbids Jenny to wear the silk, in the first place, to save the silk. She is more concerned that the fine frock shall be unspoiled than that Jenny's mind shall brace itself up to self-action. She rejuvenates it, in the second place, because she is more concerned to have the reputation of thrift with her neighbors than to have Jenny receive a thorough and wholesome lesson. Ah, the selfishness of these mothers!

Some children have what appears to be an ineradicable tendency to lateness. Whether the errand be duty or pleasure, they are always behindhand. Their parents are continually urging and reminding—drumming them up, as the phrase goes. Whether they are going to church or to school or to a pleasure-drive, the few last moments are tempestuous with hurry. Father is angry; mother is angry too, but keeps it down *because* father is, and it will never do to have both in a rage together; and for half an hour every one is nervous, flushed, and uncomfortable—and "I declare, Ella, if you can not be ready in season, I will go without you. I will not have such a fuss every time you are going any where."

Yes you will, papa, have just such a fuss; and you will not go off without her, and Ella knows it. That is just what you ought to do, but just what you will not do. Ella is fourteen years old now, and if you had been going to do it you would have done it seven years ago. And how easy a thing it is to do! You

announce at dinner that you will drive at sev-
en, and all the children who are ready then
may drive with you. Ella is of an age to take
care of herself, and you say nothing to her
about being in season. If she do not begin to
dress soon enough, you remain quiet. You do
not suggest to her that in fifteen minutes the
carriage will be here. You leave her to the
logic of events. Neither shall you be severe
and stern and virtuous, my Pharisee, who are
probably ten times worse than Ella, only there
is no one to stand over you and tell you so.
You are sunshiny and natural and affectionate ; and when seven o'clock strikes, and Ella
is rushing around frantic after her boot-but-
toner, you bid her good-by cheerily, hope you
will have her company some evening before
she is twenty-one, and drive off ; and you say
nothing about it afterward. You do not irritate her with long harangues about the evil
consequences of tardiness. A very erroneous
supposition it is that parents are to do every

thing for the children. Let them alone, and give Nature a chance. Events will train them if parents will not insist on putting their hands in and making a tangle. When Ella, left to her own devices, has lost half a dozen drives, and received half a dozen tardy marks at school, and walked six times to church, blowzy, frowzy, and alone, she will yield to the inevitableness of law, and bestir herself in season. At least I would try it.

Children ought to have a regular income while they are yet very young, certain bounds within which to spend it, perfect freedom within those bounds, and not too much advice. Children may be treated like winter rye and red-top. If you want an early field or a green lawn in spring, you need not wait till spring comes. You will then sow in uncertainty; for, with all your agricultural knowledge, you can not tell the precise time when snow and rain strike an average and the seed will be safe. You are in danger of sowing too early

and losing the seed, or sowing too late and
losing time.   But trust Nature.   Put the little
seed into the ground in the fall, and let it
judge for itself.   It will lie intact all winter
in the frozen embrace of the sod ; and, without a moment's delay or a moment's error, at
the exact time it will spring forth into glad-
ness and life.

So, if you wait and watch for the hour when
a child shall evince wisdom enough to assume
responsibility, you will scarcely hit the mark.
You will fall short or go beyond.   But give
him the responsibility outright.   His little soul
will be indifferent to it, unconscious of it, un-
harmed by it, till the fullness of time is come,
and then, without waste or hurry, it lays firm
hold of the new power.

It seems a little whimsical to attach any importance to the possession of money by children ; but money is the best teacher in the
world.   It is sure, exacting, unbending, logical.   It is the standard not only of material

but also of moral values. In one sense, a man's character may be determined by his money. He who is lax in money matters is organically lax. A man's honor never rises one sixteenth of an inch higher than his principles about debt and credit. Men and women who are careless about payments will do mean things. You may call their carelessness generosity, or high spirit, or any other fine name, but it is always capable of meanness, and it generally puts its capability into practice. This is a quality which parents ought to dig out of a child's heart, or else dig his heart out. It is only by being complete master of money that he can learn its nature and limits; and the complete mastery of a very small sum will teach him every thing he needs to know. What he needs to know is, first, intellectually the value of money; and, second, morally its uses. The little boy who has charge of his own confectionery department, with five cents a week or one cent a week for capital, is com-

passing more of prudence, economy, contriv-
ance, combination, than fifty paternal lectures
will give him. Yet I have seen girls and boys
growing up to be fourteen and fifteen years
old with no money except a chance penny, or
half a dollar on a holiday. They have every
comfort and many luxuries; what do they
want of money, which they would only spend
foolishly? Then take away some of their luxuries, give them money instead, and let them
spend it foolishly, and see what comes of it.
As it is, these children have no idea of the
value of money, or indeed of any thing else.
Consequently they are extravagant and de-
structive. They have nothing but the eye to
fix their choice. They do not know the difference between a little mischief and a great deal
of mischief. If they break your watch crystal,
they will feel as much terror as if they had
ruined your watch; and, worse than this, having no money to pay for the repair, and so
make, or at least offer, honorable reparation,

they conceal it from their parents, instinctively trusting their secret to your delicacy. So they are not only failing to prepare for a manly future, but are actually preparing for an unmanly one.

The daughter does not understand income and expenditure, and does not know how many ways there are for money to go, and how closely her mother must look at a dollar before she decides which way to start it. But the mother knows, or ought to know, how much she can afford to spend on the girl's dress. Why not give her the money, and let her spend it herself? No matter if she make mistakes. It is far better to make them now, while she has her mother for a court of last resort, than by and by, when she is called upon to act for herself, and has large interests at stake. The parents think their daughter is unreasonable in her requirements, but she is not. She has no means of knowing what is reasonable or unreasonable. She has no income, and she

can not know what expense is proportionate.
By and by, when she marries, she will be the
sort of wife that will tease her husband into
buying camel's-hair shawls and velvet carpets,
which he can not afford; and he will avenge
himself by writing a letter to the newspapers
on the extravagance of women. But women
are not really half so extravagant as men.
They will patiently and unprotestingly practice small economies which men scorn. Men
will spend recklessly for their personal comfort where women will sacrifice personal comfort altogether.

The trouble with the extravagant wife, and
with the unreasonable girl from whom she
sprang, is the same—the absence of a fixed income, and therefore any standard of expense.
Give the young girl a stated sum, and make
her responsible for her gloves, handkerchiefs,
ribbons, shoes, and, as she matures, for her
whole wardrobe. She will very soon develop
a surprising carefulness. She will be as wise

as her mother about wearing her best cream-
colored gloves in the railroad train, and as particular as her mother about folding her ribbons without crumpling, and looking after her
laces from the wash. In fact, I am sorry to
say that the beautiful daughter, the noble son,
may discover a latent meanness in connection
with their money which is appalling. The
girl who is forward to give gifts, and lavish in
expense, when she has to extract it all spas-
modically from her father, is no sooner made
mistress of an annuity than she becomes what,
if she were an old man and not a lovely young
girl, we should call miserly, greedy, cunning.
She declines to give and grudges to pay; and
in her small ribbon-y, glove-y way, tries to
overreach. Well if this quality reveal itself
under the loving mother's eye, that her loving
hand may check the hateful growth; that her
loving lips may teach, day after day, the duty
and delight of benevolence and generosity
and, first of all, uprightness.

But mothers will none of these things. They will not let their girls alone, to spend and save and suffer and grow strong. Untrustworthy race, I know what you do. You constantly interfere between cause and effect. When your daughters have spent their allowance, you make them presents. When they have run behindhand, you anticipate the next payment. When they see something more costly than their means will allow, they tease you for it, and you presently buy it. When they are suffering from a three-days' lack of money, you give them a dollar or two out of your own purse. So you destroy the only condition which gives the arrangement value, viz., unchangingness, inevitability. Whenever the law pinches, you step in and thrust it aside. But it is the pinch that enforces the law; and having done every thing you ought not to do, and left undone every thing that you ought to do, mixing up law and license, pleasure and pain, in irretrievable confusion, you fold your hands and think yourself a devoted mother. And so you are, and your children will, no doubt, one day rise up and call you blessed ; but could you not make things easier in the process?

Also should it be most thoroughly understood that this arrangement of income is merely an arrangement of common interests, and not the payment of money to a foreign power. A little girl was once alienated for life from her father because he made her wear two figs strung around her neck to punish her for having stolen them from the dinner-table. How great was her sin, or how incommensurate the punishment, history furnishes us no aggravating nor extenuating circumstances by which to judge ; but I desire to protest against the unwisdom and injustice of calling such an act stealing, or of assuming for a moment that there can be any such thing as stealing between parents and little children. It may be disobedience, and, if not suppressed, it may lead to theft—but theft it is not; and if it were, I would not let a child think so. There are pitfalls enough for his little soul to stumble into without leading him out of his path to throw him into one that he would never have found himself.

Every thing that tends to create a division of interests between parents and children should be discouraged. Every thing that tends to create unity should be fostered. It is never too early to make a child feel his ownership of home—not the ownership of tyranny and selfishness, but of affection and attachment. Let him have his share of the proprietorship in all its comforts, conveniences, luxuries, and self-denials. I do not know what the law would say, but they *are* his. The rights of a child are the strongest in the world. His absolute inability to defend them throws a sacred burden upon grown-up people. He owns every thing he is born to. The wealth of his father is his by divine right.

All that his parents can do—what they are strictly bound to do—is to pass over his property to him in such measure, by such means, as shall be most for his welfare. To talk of his stealing figs from his father's table is absurd. The table is his, figs, father, and all. He must keep his little hands off, because it is not good manners to put them on, because he will get his fingers sticky and soil his frock, because the time for figs is not yet, and he must not take his till Kate and Mary and Frank have theirs; but not in the least because the figs belong to somebody else, and not him. And if his little confused, fumbling, twilight soul half thinks it *is* stealing, does not rightly know the difference, soothe away the vagueness, or hush it away by silence. One sin at a time is enough for him to be saddled with. When he has been ordered not to touch the figs, there is a clear case of disobedience. Let it stand out by itself, not be mixed in with something else. Since nothing

G

has ever been said to him about it, wherein
does his fault consist? But children are so
conscientious that they will often show signs
of guilt when a wise man will be puzzled
to define it. The part of wisdom is not to
multiply iniquities, but to diminish them.
Bessie had contracted a habit—a mere habit—
of waking up in the night and going to her
mother's room. Presently her mother told
her she must not come into her room again
unless she were sick. The very next night I
was awakened, and aware of a little midget
pawing rapidly over the head of my bed with
speechless but ferocious resolution, and down
snuggled Bessie, not half awake, and in a minute not even that. In the morning, and in the
full possession of her senses, conscious crime
gnawed at Bessie's heart, and when she heard
her mother's step coming in search of her she
for an instant contemplated concealment. But
her mother was wise enough to pass it over
slightly, and it was with great relief that Bessie

bounced up after she was gone, and cried, "She didn't care a bit."

And Bessie was not the least harmed by it, though that evil and bitter thing, "a strict disciplinarian," might have made out a first-class case of disobedience and evasion. It was nothing of the sort. It was strict obedience and admirable invention, showing a fertility of resource while half asleep that promised well for future usefulness when wide awake.

It seems to me it is always best to make out as little sin as possible; to assume as much good intent as possible; to attribute innocent motives, and call a child good for the sake of inducing him to become so; to dispense with rules, and not make much ado about nothing. Why should a parent be constantly coming out with a command, and bringing his will face to face with his child's? It is sometimes, doubtless, unavoidable, but it is not very often. Children, as a general thing, do not need to be ordered about, or to be kept

back with a sword. They are amenable to
the law written in their hearts. They learn
very early to understand the relations of figs
and cake, and pie and preserves, if they are
treated like reasonable beings and interested
friends. But if they are put under ban; if
no confidence is reposed in them, and no dis-
cretion is expected of them; if their constitu-
tional government is simply "you shall" and
"you shall not;" if they are made to go in
leading-strings, and dainties are locked away
from them, and every thing is the property of
their parents, and they have no rights in the
sugar-bowl and jam-pot which their elders are
bound to respect, but stand on the same foot-
ing with the beggar-boy in the streets—why,
it would be very strange if they should not
steal the figs; and were the case left to me, I
should make the father wear them around his
neck, and see that the string was drawn tight
and tidy!

IV.

A MAN-CHILD.

Scene: in the country. *Dramatis personæ:* Opal, aged seven; Inspired Idiot, aged five.

OPAL (*loquitur*): "Eh! I. I., won't you feel nice by and by, when we go back to town, and you have to have a nurse following you round every where?"

I. I. feels the iron enter into his soul, but the far-off shining sun of manhood rises with healing in his wings.

"But one of these days, Opal, I shall be a big boy. I shall be thirteen years old. I shall be as big as Vaughan, and then I shall go every where. But you, Opal, you never will be a boy. You will always be a girl."

"Yes, but I sha'n't have a nurse always. I shall go by myself."

This I. I. can not gainsay, and he squares

himself as bravely as may be to endure the
degradation of a nurse. Or to fling it off.
Which shall it be? I know of a boy nine years
old who has never been out-doors in the city
without being under the eyes of his nurse.
There is a certain sense of safety and protection in this which must be very comforting to
the mother; but does it not mar self-reliance,
and irritate the love of adventure which ought
to exist in boys? The Inspired Idiot gradually wears away from the thraldom of nurse
and guardian, and fronts the world alone. A
thousand dangers menace him. He is caught
swinging under carriages in the thronged street,
and violently brought home. He strays into
horse-cars, rides into the suburbs, and is brought
back by the police. He wanders into hotels,
and motherly women lay hands upon him, and
wash his face—an attention which he seems
to consider as much in order as any other rite
of a fashionable call. Here he comes now,
swinging up the steps, overcoat unbuttoned and

flying open, cap bravely set on the back of his head, both hands in his pockets, well content with all the world.

"Eh! Opal! Yoh! See what I've bought for you! Bertha Blonde, eh!"

"But where did you get the money?"

"Mr. Olde gave it to me and all that is her dresses. Look-a-here, Opal!"

"But who is Mr. Olde? What Mr. Olde gave you the money?"

"Mr. Olde gave it to me. That's up where father is."

"How did you know his name was Olde?"

"'Cause I *know* him. I tumbled over his leg once."

This must be accepted as proof of intimacy.

"But, I. I., did you ask him for money? Beggar-boys do that."

"No, I didn't ask him, neither"—in an aggrieved tone.

"How came he to give it to you, then? Tell us all about it. Where did you see him?"

" On thavenue."

" And you went up and asked him for money ?"

" No, I didn't ask him.   He gave it to me."

" Tell me just what he said first.   Did you speak to him first, or he to you ?"

" He spoke to me.   He said what was I cry-ing for and I said a boy got my rattle-bones and he said all right and he gave me twenty-five cents."

" But where did you get your rattle-bones ?"

" I *bought* 'em."

" Where did you get that money ?"

" I got it home.   Father gave it to me and I went down street and I went into a store and I bought my rattle-bones and—"

" How much did you pay for them ?"

" Twenty-five cents and I and—look-a-here —I bought my rattle-bones and I come out and a boy came along—e-h-h"—(gasping for breath in the rapidly increasing rush of nar-rative)—" lemme tell you !—and a boy came

up and he said would I lend him my rattle-
bones and he would give me some cake and I
gave him my rattle-bones and he said he must
go round the corner and get the cake and he
took my rattle-bones and — e-h-h — he went
round the corner—OPAL, WOULD YOU RATHER
HAVE BESSY BLUE THAN BERTHA BLONDE? 'CAUSE
I'LL GO DOWN THAVENUE AND CHANGE IT!"

"No, no; never mind Bessy Blue. What
did the boy do when he got round the corner?"

"Lemme tell you! He got my rattle-bones
and he went round to get the cake and never
came back and I went round to get him and
he wasn't there and the man that had the cake
said he had not been there no more never and
—eh-h-h—he had my rattle-bones and never
came back and—HE OUGHT TO 'A TOLD ME HE'S
A THIEF!" with a sudden yell, as it dawned
upon him that he had been cheated.

"Then Mr. Olde came up, and you asked
him to give you some money, did you?"

"No, I did not ask him. Mr. Olde came

along and I was crying 'cause that boy he
didn't come back with my rattle-bones; he'd
gone off with my rattle-bones and Mr. Olde
asked me what was I crying for and I said a
boy had run off with my rattle-bones—Opal,
don't you want Bessy Blue ?"

"Yes; I said Bessy Blue all the time."

"Well, I asked for Bessy Blue and she gave
me Bertha Blonde and I didn't know 'twas
Bertha Blonde till I got home. Gimme here,
Opal; I'll go and change it."

"You said a boy had run off with your rattle-bones. What did Mr. Olde say then ?"

"And Mr. Olde said"—resuming his rapid
recitative—"Mr. Olde said he said what did
my rattle-bones cost and I said twenty-five
cents and he gave me twenty-five cents and
said go buy some more—e-h-h—and I said I
wanted to buy Opal some paper dolls too and
he said what would that cost and I said twenty-five cents and he said all right and he gave
me twenty-five cents more and I bought Opal's

paper doll. I asked for Bessy Blue—e-h-h—
and she gave me Bertha Blonde and it was
dark and I couldn't see till I got 'most home
and I couldn't go back to buy my rattle-bones
'cause 'twas too far and Mr. Olde said all right
and I've got my quarter, I've got him! There
he is!" brandishing his scrip aloft with a shout
of exultation.

"And then you came directly home alone?"

"No, Mr. Olde came with me. And I went
into a store with him like where you go, mamma. I have been there with you, mamma."

"Did Mr. Olde ask you to go in with him?"

"No; a man came out and made him go in
and me. And he gave him some Champagne
and me too and I tasted it and I did not like
it and then he gave me some more and I did
not like that either and I said that wasn't the
Champagne my father drinks and he said 'Try
him with the sherry' and I did not like that
either and they laughed and then we came
home and Mr. Olde went to the Clarendon and

he said 'Now you know the way home?' and I
said yes. Hoh! jus' if I didn't know the way
home!"

And now approaches bed-time for the Inspired Idiot. Repeatedly during dinner, when
he is tired of swallowing, has he plumped his
head deep down into the folds of his mother's
dress to rest and refresh himself for new de-
glutitory efforts. After dinner he deploys on
two chairs, or on the floor, it may be, in an ecstasy of flatness. But when he goes up to bed
his spirits revive. He kicks off first one shoe,
then the other, and runs a race around the
room in his stockings. Then he is moved with
reminiscences of the marionettes, and he tells
you how the Punch or some other puppet fell
from a great height and was broken to pieces,
and then gathered himself together, and " he
rose and he rose and he rose till he had as
many *roses* as there were before!" He is seized
also with the spirit of prophecy, and glows
with the guns and swords and ponies that he

is speedily to become possessed of, and which
gradually mount from one of each kind for
himself to a thoroughly equipped cavalry force
ready for battle. "And won't my pony look
funny when he sees me coming?"

And now the outer layer of integuments is
cajoled off, and he stands in the *déshabillé* of
Angola, eloquent and gesticulating, till the
sprite of fun and frolic comes upon him, and
he canters about the room once more, jumps
upon the sofa, buries himself among the pillows, kicks up first one little red leg and then
another, and only regrets that the supply ceases
so soon; and finally consents to have the rabbit skinned, but with a demure and watchful
look during the process, which shows that the
rabbit must be closely watched, for he does
not mean to rehabilitate himself when he is
skinned, but to take a leap and a turn around
the room in all the freedom of Parádise.

And so presently the Inspired Idiot stands
all white-robed and clean and sweet and still,

ready for the most earnest talk about things in
heaven or earth or under the earth.   His final
fancy is to give a party, to which who shall be
invited—Bertie Fletcher ?

"Oh no, mamma; because he wears a kilt,
and all the boys would think he was a girl and
would not play with him !"

"Is that so ?   I suppose, of course, you will
invite Stephen Stetson."

"No, I can't have Stephie Stetson because
he is a naughty boy.   He curses and swears."

"I. I., what do you mean by cursing and
swearing ?   What is it to swear ?"

"It is"—in a hushed, reverent voice—
"why, it is to say God out of your prayers !"

But the worst of it is that the Inspired Idiot
is not exempt from the evils of life ; but just
as painfully as the rest of us he must pay the
penalty of nature's violated laws ; so he moans
out of his sleep with the toothache, and is ef-
fectually aroused by mighty pangs quite out
of proportion with the tiny tooth that causes

them. He has sense enough not to increase
the trouble by trying to bear it in silence, and
shrieks and wails relieve his burdened nerves.

"I never will forgive God for this," he cries,
outraged and indignant, in the midst of his
paroxysms. "I never *will* forgive God for
this."

It is a living and logical faith, however er-
ratic in its philosophy.

"But I don't think God is to blame for it,"
suggests an older and perhaps a wiser head.

"Who is, then?" asks I. I., opening to a new
idea.

"Little I. I., who stayed out in the cold too
long and too late."

And then another pang arises, stronger than
the last, and he flings himself down to the foot
of the bed, and shouts, "Now I am *mad!*"

Poor little Inspired Idiot, grappling with
feeble hands the great question of the origin
of evil, bearing with questionable fortitude the
fangs of evil itself, a little salt and soothing

will lull your rebellion to sleep, but neither
you nor I can go far in the wrong direction
without running against the Almighty, even
upon the thick bosses of his bucklers. We
may believe in his goodness, but we are certain of his power.

By and by, when all has long been still, and
care-takers have departed, a voice is heard—
"Mamma, come up stairs!" A white figure
stands sturdy and smiling at the head of the
staircase. "Mamma, I heard it was ten o'clock,
so I got up to take my med'cine, and I spilt it
on my night-gown." Then as he sits warm-
ing, drying, and comfortable before the fire,
thus he muses:

"Think I'll die, mamma?"

"What makes you think of dying?"

"'Cause I didn't take my med'cine. I spilt
it."

"Oh no! I don't think you will die for
that."

A pause.

"Think I won't die, then?"

"Not at all."

"How will I see heaven, then?"

"But you don't want to die, do you?"

"No"—hesitatingly; "but I should like to see heaven."

Another long pause.

"If I should get a very long ladder, couldn't I go up and look into heaven?"

"No."

"If I should get a hundred and thirty ladders, couldn't I?"

"No."

"If I should get all the ladders in all the world, in all the countries, and tie them one atop of another, couldn't I climb up and just peek in?"

"No."

"Why couldn't I, mamma? Give a reason."

"Because you would be dizzy and fall down!"

H

Go your ways, Inspired Idiot, man-child—
tiny package of loves and hates and hopes and
fears; timorous where helplessness itself is
safe, and brave where the boldest quail; peering with calm eyes into unfathomable mysteries; treading with equally serene feet the
valley of the shadow of death and the remot-
est fastnesses of life; filled with great longings
for airy nothings, and violent passions over
petty grievances, and deep interests in passing
trifles; boisterous and ineffably gentle; breezy
and noisy and riotous, yet tender and nestling
and delicate and soft; ignorant and wise;
blind and baffled, yet shrewd and far-seeing;
pliant to a word, a touch, a look, a hint, yet as
firm and fixed, as clearly outlined and as steadily set, as the veriest patriarch of the nations!
I wonder if Eve knew all she said when she
looked upon her queer, new, first little man,
and solemnly concluded her marveling meditations—"I have gotten a man from the
Lord!"

V.

THE CHILDREN OF THE CHURCH.

"Give a dog a bad name and kill him."
It is a rough phrase, but it lives because it embodies a vital truth.   Nor is the truth confined
to dogs, nor even primarily spoken of dogs;
but, as Paul might say, it was written altogether for our sakes.

A little child is born, innocent of theology,
theoretically unacquainted with God, absolutely ignorant, and practically helpless in mind,
body, and estate.   If his parents are thieves,
murderers, adulterers, profane swearers, drunkards, liars, there is a sad probability that he will
become like them.   If they fear God and walk
in his ways, is there not a probability that the
child will accompany them?   Is it not their
duty to assume that he will?

It seems to me a real and serious defect in

our orthodox polity or doctrine—whichever it is—that we give the children of the Church no advantage over the children of this world. On the contrary, they are almost under a disadvantage. The little victims of the slums and alleys will be lost, indeed; but their ignorance will be a mitigation of their punishment, whereas the children of the Church will suffer the added poignancy of the sermons, the songs, the prayers, the teachings which they have heard and withstood. We assume, not the non-transmissibility of moral qualities, but the transmissibility of immoral qualities. In Adam we involuntarily died; but in Christ none are made alive except by their own act. The sins of the parents are visited upon the children; but their virtues stop with themselves. The children of parents who are friends of God must go through the same processes of conviction of sin and conversion to holiness as the children of those who are haters of God or unacquainted with his name. Mental culture

changes the plane of life ; but moral and religious culture permits each generation to begin where its predecessor began. Every child,
alike of Christian as of heathen parents, is born
under the divine displeasure.

Did my ears deceive me ? I was at a council convened for the purpose of inquiring into
the disputed faith of a brother suspected of
heretical tendencies. A paper was read in
which he presented his creed ; and in this paper he announced his belief that we were all
" born under the divine displeasure." He was
ejected from the council; though I can not
affirm that this clause of his creed was, as it
should have been, the immediate disposing
cause.

What is meant by being born under the divine displeasure ? Which does sin, the child
or his parents ? When people who are thrift-
less, shiftless, incapable of taking care of themselves, quarrelsome, unprincipled, and wretched introduce into the world a living soul, for

whom they are unable to make any adequate
provision, one can understand that they should
incur the divine displeasure. But when a husband and wife who love each other become the
delighted parents of a child, for whose comfort, happiness, and welfare they are able and
eager to provide, and on whom they lavish
their best, why should the divine displeasure
alight on them? What law have they violated? what crime committed?

Or is it the poor little baby with whom God
is angry? Is there any council or any collec-
tion of grown men who will venture to affirm
that any sentient being in the heavens above
or the earth beneath can view with a harsher
feeling than profound compassion this helpless,
unconscious little creature, born to its certain
troubles and to its only possible joys? The
great God displeased with a baby! "And Jesus called a little child unto him, and set him
in the midst of them;" and when he had taken
him in his arms, he said unto them: "Except

ye be converted and become as little children, ye shall not enter into the kingdom of heaven." How many heretics must agree, how many councils must announce that we are born under the divine displeasure, to neutralize the impression produced by Jesus Christ calling, caressing, blessing the little children?

If he is not displeased with the father and mother for being the parents of a child, nor with the child for being born, with whom is he displeased? Not with the general system under which such things happen, for it is his own institution. The mother might show good cause for displeasure; but that an Omnipotent Being should have ordered the issues of life just as they are, and then be in a state of constant displeasure with them, seems absurd.

I suppose the words are susceptible of some interpretation or explanation which shall render them intelligible and acceptable to the rational mind; but in their simple, natural meaning, can the rational mind do any thing but reject them? As such words are used in the common language of the earth, they seem utterly false, derogatory to the divine character, and cruelly adapted to widen the breach between man and his Maker. So far is it from being true that we are born under the divine displeasure, I should rather say the one thing God can not be angry with us for is being born. Little children are under his peculiar patronage. Even when he is justly displeased with parents for their inconsiderate, selfish, wicked introduction of a fresh life to fresh sorrow, he can have only the deepest pity and love for the wretched little victim. And for the rest, for the honest, virtuous, thrifty Christian parents—to whom every child is a new incentive to love, a new development of grace, a new hold on life and hope—are not their children born under the very smile of God? Sees he not in every opening life the perfect working of his plans, a gentle unfolding of power, another centre of happiness ?

Teach children from their infancy that they are carnally minded, at enmity with God, and that they need reconciliation with him, and doubtless after a while your teachings will be literally true. But why should not children be brought up from the beginning on good terms with their Maker? They are not naturally hostile to him. So far as I have seen children, they are naturally reverent, dutifully and even affectionately disposed toward God. They do not need reconciliation to him, for they have never quarreled with him. They need constant enlightenment, constant guidance, constant repression, it may be, and encouragement; for they are weak and wild. But surely their dutiful and affectionate disposition toward God ought to be recognized and cultivated. It should be assumed at the outset that they are his children, consecrated to him by the word, the deed, the very nature

of their parents, bound to him by their own
natural love and liking. They have not to be
converted to him, any more than they have to
their parents. He *is* their most loving parent,
whom they love as fast as they learn. They
will often sin against him, as they often sin
against their father and mother. But from
the little outbursts of childish rebellion, impatience, or fatigue, we do not infer a state of
continuous hatred to the mother. Why should
we infer a state of hatred to God ? The anger and the petulance, even the disobedience,
are not the rule, but the deviations from the
rule. They are not because the child hates
his parents, but because swift and sudden
temptations overbear his sense of duty. All
the way along, through the thick of his worst
actions, his love maintains its strong and
steady current, strengthening with his strength,
growing clear and calm and pure as he in-
creases in wisdom and stature, and never losing itself even when it mingles with the waters of the river of life.

So let the little child be taught to love God
—not against, but in unison with his nature.
Let him be taught to consider himself a Christian from the beginning—a little Christian, to
be sure, but a little Christian; not a little Pagan, not a little worldling. His lapses into
sin—that is, into crossness and lies and disobedience and untidiness and carelessness — are
beneath his standard, against his principles,
contrary to his designs. He shall be helped
by prayer and praise, and punishment, if need
be, to overcome his faults; but he shall not be
drummed out of the ranks on account of them.
We, his elders, are cross and careless. We tell
lies, and we are selfish and impatient and inconsiderate; but we account ourselves Christians for all that. Shall we be harder on the
little men and women, who stand in their little
places and do deeds of heroism in the way of
self-culture and repression of bad habits, who
make little martyrs of themselves, and become
little saints over their dolls and hoops and

tarts ? " Take heed that ye despise not one of
these little ones; for I say unto you that in
heaven their angels do always behold the face
of my Father which is in heaven."

We should naturally suppose that the claims
of God upon man would be expressed in terms
as sensible, simple, and intelligible as those
which embody any earthly duty. It requires
a certain degree of intellect to be a statesman,
a lawyer, a tradesman, a teacher, a farmer, a
mechanic. But all men are not required to
be lawyers or mechanics. There are many
men, women, and children whose duties range
downward in simplicity, till they almost reach
the level of the poet's little maiden, who

> " Knew no sterner duty
> Than to give caresses."

But no man lives so low as not to owe obligation to his Maker. So soon as the first divine
ray glimmers into the little heart, so soon
should that heart open to its shining. Religion is universal in its demands. All need to

be bound each day anew and afresh to their
Creator, their Preserver, their bountiful Bene-
factor.

We should infer, therefore, that the divine
claims would be presented so plainly that all
could understand them—not simply ministers
and lawyers and men skilled in language and
philosophy, but the unlearned and the un-
stable.

It seems to me that they are so; but that we
overlay them with our many comments and
deductions and directions, till their clearness
is shrouded in obscurity. God in the Holy
Bible, in the human heart, in nature, and in
society reveals to us his will with great directness and distinctness; but we are very apt to
make the Word of God of none effect by our
traditions, and his logic equally inconsequent
by our prejudices. The divine Word is not
nearly so hard to understand as the human
words that are written in explanation of it.

A paragraph clipped from a religious pa-

per, under the heading "I'm lost! I'm lost!"
explains that "this exclamation was overheard,
lately, by a pastor as he entered the chamber
of a Sunday-school boy, thirteen years old, who
had been suddenly taken ill and pronounced
by his physician irrecoverable. He had, as
others, been taught his duty, and the fond in-
vitations and solemn expostulations of the dear
Redeemer; but, under the delusion that there
was *time enough* for repentance, he had lived
regardless, until, thus unexpectedly cast upon
his death-bed, he was alarmed with the consciousness that 'the harvest was past, the summer was ended,' and he was not saved! The
pastor prayed, and tried to impress him with
the love of Jesus; and he, endeavoring to grasp
it as the drowning person catches at an object, appeared to take comfort. But oh! how
earnestly he exhorted father, grandfather, and
brothers not to delay repentance! Whether
he obtained saving grace or not will be known
at the 'dread tribunal.' "

Such a story as this, so far from inspiring one with any sense of greater responsibility or more solemn urgency, rather arouses a certain indignation against those whose teachings can inflict such anguish upon a child. It is not so much the parents who are to blame. Perhaps no one is to be severely blamed for willful perversion of the truth or malice toward the helpless. But surely those who, no doubt conscientiously, take it upon themselves to be expounders of truth, ought to be thoughtful enough and real enough to give us at least a common-sense view of common events.

Among all our teachers and preachers, in pulpit and press, is there nobody to tell us that the distress of this poor little boy was no indi- cation of the truth of the doctrine which dis- tressed him ? His agony had no bearing what- ever upon his fate, and little upon his charac- ter. It did not signify that he was lost, or that he was a sinner; but only that he had been trained to believe that, unless he went

through a certain definite moral or mental
process, of which probably the poor little fellow had but the most vague conception, he
would suffer inconceivable torment forever.
The state of mind of a person on his death-bed
is significant, in a certain measure, of his character, largely of his temperament, his training, and his beliefs ; but it is no trustworthy
witness of abstract truth.   A man, devout, spiritual, sweet, is consoled by the promises of the
Gospel, which in health was his meat day and
night.   A man who never cared for Christ,
but whose chief aim was to accumulate property, is comforted by the thought of the immense fortune he leaves behind him, and dies
as peacefully and calmly as his Christian
brother.   If the experience of the first is a
proof of the truth of the Gospel, the experience of the second is a proof of the excellence
of gain as the guide of life.   A religious newspaper lately told of a man who had been under strong convictions of sin, but who had re-

sisted the call to repentance, until suddenly his
agitation and anxiety subsided into a strange
calm that was not peace.   He felt that the
Holy Spirit had ceased to strive with him,
that he was given over to eternal death; but
kept on the even tenor of his way, without
hope, yet without tumultuous fear.   After
several years his mood changed, and he became a Christian.   Now if at any time between the advent and the disappearance of
this sudden calm despair this man had met a
swift death, he would have been considered
lost by all who were acquainted with his peculiar case.   It would have been said that he
resisted the Spirit, and on such a date the
Spirit departed from him forever, and his
doom was sealed.   But as he lived, there was
space to show that for all those years even the
man's own opinion of himself was wrong.   He
was not doomed to eternal death.   The Spirit
had not given up striving with him.   This little boy on his death-bed was no more sure

I

that he was lost than the strong man in his strength. But the strong man was saved in his despair, and the little boy was not lost for his.

Observe, it is nowhere implied that this boy was a bad boy. He was a Sunday-school scholar; he was certainly in a degree unselfish, for, though fearing the worst fate for himself, he was eager that his friends should escape it. He was docile; he accepted with pathetic, unquestioning trust the doctrines which had been delivered to him, even though they consigned him to the pains of hell forever. All that is alleged against him is that he had lived regardless of repentance. But he was thirteen years old. Look at a boy thirteen years old. How full of adventure and experiment he is! how ambitious, how resolute, how little introspective, and of his little introspection how shy and reticent! Preach to such a boy our vague metaphysical ecclesiastical repentance, and what does he know about it all when you are through? He knows what bitter regret for a mean act is; he knows the poignancy of disappointment and the shame of failure. With the fashions and passions of his boy-world he is familiar; but when you involve yourself in clouds, and talk to him in abstract cloud-language, your words are as idle tales. I believe that many conscientious children are more pained and bewildered than benefited by the well-meant but indefinite and terrifying teachings of their elders. They feel that a dreadful doom impends, which they know not how to escape. To be truthful, kind, obedient, avails them nothing; there must be some inward change, some subjective mental process, which they can neither compass nor comprehend. Either they give in to it, and grow morbid and timid, and suffer unknown agonies of apprehension, or they throw it off, and undergo a hardening process, by which they become impervious alike to truth and error.

It is of little use to preach to children sorrow for sin. If they can be made to feel sorry for sins, it is all we have a right to expect. If we believe that God is their Father, why not believe that he acts on fatherly principles? We know very little about the future; but we know of a surety that honor and honesty and truth and love are the best possessions in this world, and they can not harm us in the next. Why should not a child be taught that his Father in heaven wants of him just what his father on earth wants—that he should learn his lessons, and be polite to his teachers, and fair in his games, and dutiful to his parents, and friendly to all; that repentance means only that he should not exult in wrong-doing, but regret it and try to do so no more, and make it the rule and study of his life to do the upright, the just, the high-minded thing, instead of the doubtful and despicable one? How can he love God, whom he hath not seen, except through the friends whom he hath seen?

Why did God devise this most intricate and elaborate scheme of the human family, but for the express purpose of leading the rude, ignorant soul with sweet, slow steps, through all the gradations of animal instincts and human loves up to his own infinite love?   Fathers and mothers, teachers and preachers, can clear the way for his inexperienced feet by simply giving him true ideas of his position, of the relation in which he stands to his Creator, of the entire, the rational friendliness and sympathy with which his Maker regards him.   Or they can confuse and confound him with their abstractions and their inconsequences.   It is difficult to be angry, for the sword pierces through their own souls also.   It is difficult not to be angry, for the unspeakable and immeasurable woe is caused by the perversion of truth in those whose duty it is to present truth.

VI.

LESSONS TO BE LEARNED FROM THE YOUNG REPUBLIC.

CHILDREN are no doubt tiresome to people who have the care of them, but irresponsible association with children is a never-ceasing interest and delight. To sit alone in the park and study the different groups of little ones playing about you is at once employment and enjoyment. The flossy, flowing hair, the Vandyke collars, the dainty, diminutive petticoats, the broad sashes, the Tyrolese hats, the shapely legs, the free, visible motions, the infinite flashing of vivid colors—here is a little picturesque world within the world, not less real and far more accessible than the outer world which infolds it. Have the mothers given too much time to tucks and trimmings? I dare say they have, the vain, fond, silly mothers,

but they have made a pretty picture after all.
And if the painter is praised who spends his
time in tricking out canvas with color and
contour to delight the eye and inthrall the
heart, shall the mother be harshly blamed
even if she trim the midnight lamp to deck
with freshness and softness and brightness that
little living statue, rounded and rosy, as fair
and pure and sweet as if it had been carved
from vitalized marble ?·

True, this picture is for a day, and the painting and the sculpture are for all time. But so
the flowers spring as gracefully outlined, as
exquisitely tinted, as lavishly dowered with
the sweet mystery and ministry of scents, as
if they were not to yield up their lovely life in
a night. All the year waits on one moment
of superb and supreme beauty. Nay, a hundred years serve steadfastly for one brief blos-
soming, and we do not chide Nature for the
lavish outlay, but admire her patience and ap-
plaud her accomplishment. The picturesque

childhood passes so swiftly, and the bright colors must be subdued and the charming outlines hidden—we may pity if we must, but not too severely censure the poetry, the love of art, the refinement and delicacy, which find expression while they may in a child's dress.

And if the heavens are shrouded as on this bitter spring day, and the air is full of invisible ice, what substitute for sunshine is so bright as the faces and the voices of the eager, busy children ? You sit by the glowing grate with an entertaining book, but "keeping an eye out," yes, and an ear too, for the microcosm in the other corner. And if you can but furnish a little wisdom of your own, you will find as much wisdom there as in any book. There, in little, all the large world reveals itself. There the future is forecast. The present holds the germ of all that is to be. It wants only the seeing eye. Life is strictly logical, but we fail to frame the syllogisms, and stand astonished at the conclusions. All the same they are conclusions, and not caprices.

There are many arrangements in the world that we can not understand; but involuntarily watching the children at their play, we can readily see why they are arranged in groups, and not consigned to solitary education. It is not alone for enjoyment, but for training. Parents do their part, but they can not do the whole. Children must themselves complement their own development. Even the defects of parental training may be made up by the inevitable trituration of these atoms. The parents are strong and self-possessed, protecting and just and friendly; but when the child goes out into the world he will find it indifferent, unjust, reckless. How can he bear the transition from the warm atmosphere of home to the cool, not to say biting airs of this new sphere? But the wise, self-restrained, helping adults do not constitute all of home. Again and again comes a little baby, more helpless, ignorant, appealing than the helpless, ignorant, and appealing child. The three-year-

old immediately constitutes herself a Mother
Superior to the three-day-old. The same lovely, helpful traits which she calls forth in her
parents the baby calls forth in her. Children
are to each other what the outside world is to
their parents. Heedless, headlong children
become careful and cautious when the baby
wanders into their play-ground. The boy who
howls and storms and raves because his mother will not yield to his wish and whim, will
himself yield to the whims of the tiny sister
left awhile in his charge, and coax and ca-
jole, not only with marvelous patience, but
with a wisdom and a tact of which you had
never suspected him to be capable. Chil
dren have an unconscious confidence in their
parents and elders, and an unconscious and
correct lack of confidence in their younger
friends. They will be unreasonable with their
parents, knowing that their parents will not be
unrestrained in return ; but when little Peggy
totters about among the infantile crockery,

they know it is of no use to thrust her out
fiercely, because no shame will restrain her
from pushing unearthly yells which will spoil
their sport. So they check their impatience,
lure her out lovingly, and learn the valuable
art of self-government.

Thank Heaven for the quarrels of children!
Thus they learn the balance of power before
they leave the nursery. Perhaps his father
will not allow Charley to be punished, but if
he strike Kitty, Kitty strikes back, and with
blind fury. So he learns to curb his tempers
in spite of his father. The trouble is that parents too often interfere when it would be much
better to leave the children to fight it out. But
Charley is stronger than Kitty, and hurts her.
True, but it is very important that Kitty should
learn to measure herself, and to know that if
she fling herself rashly against a superior
power she will be beaten. Beyond keeping a
general supervision of eyes and bones, let us
not exercise too close a watch. The outcry

and clamor are not soothing or musical considered merely as sounds, but when you classify them as the friction of souls striving to adjust themselves to the relations of life, they are far from annoying. Let the children alone. The brother's impatience may better discipline the offender than the father's patience. The sister's quick, effective resentment is more like the world's ways than the mother's loving endurance. The slap that promptly follows encroachment is a good practical lesson in human rights. Be not too hasty to forbid the little children to beat and box and tease and scold and scratch each other into a respect for ownership, for sensitiveness, into a dignified self-control, and even, at length, into a profound and universal benevolence.

An absolute monarchy may give more social order, but a republic makes stronger men and women for citizens.

When young King Philip—I refer now not to him of Pokanoket, Prince of the Wampa-

noags, son of our old friend Massasoit, but to
Philip, my king—when this youthful monarch
put on his first jacket and trousers he signal-
ized his sovereignty by striking an attitude.
Out went his feet as widely apart as his small
legs could conveniently allow, deep went his
lordly hands into his diminutive but sufficient
pockets, and up tossed his shining head, as
bright and fine and yellow with its lustrous
hair as the silken summer maize. So there he
stood- and, caught by the cunning sun, there
he still stands, a demure little mockery of a
man, a caricature of strength and dominion, a
puny baby, but mighty with the foreshadow-
ings of fate—not ridiculous, because altogether transparent and innocent, and because altogether certain in his promise.

For the king will never go back again under
petticoat government. Once a boy, always a
boy, until he is, better still, a man. No drag-
gling of draperies for him through rain or hail,
or fire or snow. No beating against the wind

with sails full spread. He goes through life
close reefed, all the hinderances of friction reduced to their lowest terms. He runs the race
without carrying weight. He rejoices in he
knows not what. It is a greater freedom than
he comprehends.

But look you, my lord, power brings duty.
We shall expect you to use your freedom.
What avails that you are girded for the race,
armed for the fight, if you fail in the one or
flee from the other? Dress is a significant,
not a merely capricious fact. From time to
time benevolent men and enterprising women
have attempted to change national customs and
costumes, and here and there a brave Bloomer
has crooked the pregnant hinges of the knee
before the public gaze; but in vain. No confessed convenience, no considerations of health
even, have been able to banish or materially to
modify the flowing female drapery. It is felt
to be not simply female, but feminine, and
even now it is a hand-to-hand conflict between

skirts that "just clear the ground" and skirts that drag their slow lengths over it. A merciful Providence save us from being conquered by the last alternative!—though to any person who sees a dress trailing over the pavements, with its intricate pleats and puffings well grimed, its protecting wigan flounce gray with dirt, or, as these eyes have seen, torn off and hopping behind, half a yard of narrow rag, a train not provided for in any fashion plate to such, I say, it might seem as if Providence had no call to interfere. We might provide against this degrading display and this untidy consciousness by our own common-sense.

But obstinate adherence to an inconvenient dress means something. Men have not so clung to it. Men by whole nations and whole races have cast aside the flowing folds which women not only retain but multiply. Visiting lately in China, I was struck anew by the similarity between the dresses of our male and female friends. Our host was equipped in a short, loose black satin sack and petticoat. His queue was less luxuriant than the ladies' hair, and his stout English boots beneath his petticoat, unlike little mice, much more like very large rats, stole in and out. His raiment was plain, whereas the silk robes of his family were rich and varied in color, and heavy with gay and golden embroidery. Otherwise their dresses were generally the same. Doubtless the Chinese eye saw a great difference in cut and fit, but to me the fullness, the length, the outline were one. The resemblance was far greater than the difference.

Here, then, we have a female dress more comfortable than our own—loose, light, and not ungraceful; as modest as our own, as rich as our own, far more permanent, and necessarily more economical. Such a dress as this must give women greater freedom of motion, and must be therefore more conducive to health. It must require far less time and thought in its construction, and therefore leaves the mind at liberty to range in other fields. The man's dress, on the contrary, is less adapted to work than the English male dress. The Celestial gentleman would seem to be as much hampered by his clothes as the Celestial lady. While relinquishing beauty, he has not gained freedom. The husband is really worse off than his wife.

Our international diversities go further than this. Our American women do not live too much in the open air; but, if we may accept the truth of history and tradition, they are in it far more than the Chinese women. They are not very accurate or profound scholars, but there is among them more intellectual depth and activity, it is generally believed, than among Chinese women. That is, the dress which we all agree is the most sensible and comfortable, and which some of us are ready to fight for, and a faithful few to suffer martyrdom on account of—the dress which gives most scope to mind and body—is worn by a

K

race proverbially circumscribed in both; while
the most impeding and absorbing dress ever
devised is worn by a race of women who stand
relatively higher than any other on earth.

There are ever so many morals fluttering
from this fact as naturally as the tail from a
kite. But as space and time are limited, suppose we confine ourselves to one. It may not
be the right one, but I should like to see some
person bring forward a better.

The spontaneous and increasing difference
between the male and female dress marks the
growth of a nation in higher civilization, and
points to the different work of man and woman. In the beginning of things there is a general commingling, a chaos of individualities
and offices. Woman is but an inferior sort of
man, always more weak, sometimes more beautiful. The distinctions of nature are imperious, but have no significance beyond their existence. Women do pretty much the same
work as men, and wear pretty much the same

dress. At the worst they are low, at the best
they are not high. But rising in the scale, the
dividing line defines itself more and more
sharply. The man's world evolves itself, rough
and palpable, from the chaos; the woman's
world, too, floats into the finer light, less pal
pable, but not less real. For his world and
work the man folds away his delaying draperies, and arrays himself in compact and en-
during substance; for her world the woman as
instinctively and unerringly wraps herself in
intricacy, voluminousness, and beauty—unerringly, because she is none the less accoutred
for her world in being encumbered for his.
The higher the man, the higher the nation, the
higher the civilization—the more he takes upon
his own brawny shoulders the pioneer toil, and
reserves her for the secondary, the social, the
invisible, the all-pervading.

So, dear lady, though your dress may be a
little in advance of your life, though you may
have put on the attire of the future while yet

under the yoke of the lingering and brutal
past, take courage. You suffer and are hin-
dered, but you are in the line of promotion.
Let Philip your king rejoice in his *propria
quæ maribus*, for that way conflict and victory lie for him. But when your clean soul is
vexed that you can not preserve your spotless dress for much sweeping and dusting and
dish-washing, rejoice over the coming woman, whose feet are already beautiful upon the
mountains, and whose sole house-cleaning
shall be to keep the chambers of the heart
—all hearts—pure and fresh and fragrant.

When Truth says, confidently, "Work"—
meaning physical labor—"is not for women,"
Incredulity replies, Yankee-like, "How are
you going to help it?" and Truth, being truthful, must reply, "I don't know;" but, just the
same, she goes on, calm and confident, singing
her eternal song, "For woman tranquillity,
leisure, large spheres, and social and mental
scope."

There is a great deal to be done, and, alas! a great deal to be suffered, before those larger spheres swing into reach; but much is gained if women, while toiling and moiling in the swamp-lands of the lower world, can hear far off their majestic music, or even know that somewhere in the circling heavens they are sweeping on to sure attainment. Work, work, work—from weary chime to chime—but, all the same, the true life is to live not according to your necessities, but according to your aspirations; to live not in constant repression, but in constant growth; to work not by will, but by instinct; to do what you must, not from outward force, but inward fervor.

It is no argument against success that you see not how it is to be accomplished. Settle what success is to be, and then work up to it. The children are brimful of lessons in the way to do it. Star-flower is the most useless little blossom that ever opened, and no queen is more loyally attended. Baby-in-breeches never

earned a pinch of salt, yet he is the very salt
of the earth.   When Star-flower presents herself at the door, blooming from her bath, her
face radiates smiles over all the universe at
the welcome she is going to receive, although
not a word is spoken, nor perhaps a look cast
in her direction.   Her confident soul plucks
its triumph beforehand.   She assumes fidelity
and homage, and is never disappointed.   She
has no self-conceit; is not concerned with the
impression she produces; is intent only on ac-
complishing her objects.   What if her single-
mindedness and simple faith could go on
through life?   What if she could rise upon
the world each morning, as smiling, as un-
daunted, as straightforward, as unsuspecting?
What if she could always be content to be,
and leave to the hard, striving, masculine
world the task to know?

Or look again: the strong man armed
comes into the room, and Little Breeches,
aware what such shoulders were made for,

climbs by short and easy stages to a seat thereon, and rides aloft in triumphant silence. Star-flower, peering amid the forbidden ruins of the overturned work-basket, suddenly catches a glimpse of the performance, and immediately her soul rises above rubbish; by vigorous use of her two little hands, and an emphatic double back-action, she gains her two little feet, trots out to front the centaur, stretches up her chubby arms and steepest tiptoes, and with an inarticulate but most significant outcry of mingled entreaty and imperiousness, claims her right to the other shoulder. Perched on the desired summit, peace settles on her brow, joy shines in her eyes, and riding up and down beneath the chandeliers, she coos out an *Io triumphe* as soft and sweet as the gurgling of a hidden brook in the leafy woods of June.

That is all she wants — her share of the goods of life. She claims no pre-eminence, only her portion. When Little Breeches de-

scends, she writhes spontaneously downward.
When Little Breeches does not mount, the
shoulders are free from her incursions. But
the altitude and the freedom that please him,
by that token please her, and with no thought
of propriety, and no drawback from consequences, she asserts herself, and is not only
justified but glorified.

Now if Star-flower will but bloom into her
womanhood, and glow through her womanhood, on the same direct and simple principle,
how fragrant will be the hedge-row where
she springs! Not submission, not aggression,
neither self-surrender nor self-obtrusion, but
clearness to see and quickness to claim, and
resolution to secure and grace to compel, what
is by divine right and human courtesy hers,
and what it is to the world's enjoyment and
advantage to award: for the whole house is
brightened and bettered because Star-flower
will have the other shoulder!

Will it make her selfish and exacting? Is

it for a woman to be always withdrawing herself to the centre of obscuration lest she be
relegated thither by force of dislike? Why,
look at Star-flower again. "Come to me, Star-
flower — come to me!" says Little Breeches,
standing across the room, and bending toward
her with outstretched arms, all the command-
ing sweetness of love in his tender voice; and
as it was in the beginning, is now, and ever
shall be, world without end, the little willful
woman hears and heeds the tone of love, and
speeds swiftly to the close-clasping arms of the
little man, and all their joy bubbles up in
merry, musical laughter. Submission, obedience, duty, subordination — no, it is none of
these; let not such things be once named
among you, as becometh saints. It is something better. It is spontaneity reaching far-
ther toward the heavenly goal than duty can
ever be spurred. Ah! be sure, with all her
ignorance, Star-flower knows what is what.
She has never mapped out her course but by

the divine instinct, as yet unwarped; she
knows when to impel and when to accord—
and her following is all the dearer because
she is not slow to lead. Perhaps when Star-
flower grows a woman, the woman-world will
be but little easier than now, but I think it
will be that little easier. The only peace of
the present is the fore-gleam of that tranquil
future. There needs only to be the same rate
of progress as in the past, and we can see that
the millennium is not unattainable, even in this
world. By the conquests of mechanical power
many a burden has been lifted from both men
and women. It is not a heroic, not a poetical,
but it is a very effective way of overcoming
the world. It is difficult to find romance in a
cheese factory, but a cheese factory lightens
the load on many a weary shoulder. When
we look back and see how much used to be
done in every house by one woman's hands
that is now done in one house by many iron
fingers, from how many forms of manual serv-

ice the poorest women are now freed, is it Quixotic to think that ingenuity is not yet exhausted? Since man has already taken upon his own hand, still more upon his own brain, so much of the work that used to weigh upon women, is it idle to think that he will go on assuming, devising, combining, through the slow, swift years, till, silently, a revolution is accomplished, and without sound of hammer or axe, without so much as intent of reconstruction, but only by the instinctive working out of destiny—the man his, and the woman hers—behold, a new heaven and a new earth, wherein dwelleth righteousness!

VII.

WHAT ENEMY HATH DONE THIS?

SOME observing father in Boston has been circulating a petition asking that the Saturday session of the Latin School in that city be abolished, and finds himself at once set up as the standard-bearer of an army which is to rescue our children from the clutches of their oppressors. Vigorous pens are set in motion. All the horrors of overtasked brains, multiplied lessons, too many hours in school, too many studies out of school, unventilated rooms, and premature disease and death are pointed out, and parents are called upon to rise in their might and demand a redress of all these grievances, or threaten a withdrawal of their children from " your schools."

The situation is grotesque, though the evil is as real as sin. Whose schools, pray, are

they from which the children are to be with-
drawn in default of a reformation? Who
prescribes the curriculum of study? Who
appoints the school-hours? Who limits the
vacations? Who builds the school-houses?
There would seem to be a vague notion afloat
that the teacher is the absolute despot who is
to be brought to terms by armed revolution.
He it is who imposes tasks so severe as to
soften the brains of his innocent charges, and
who sucks all the oxygen out of the air before he permits them to breathe it. He is the
cruel, exacting, irresponsible tyrant, tramping
to his goal over the brains of the helpless,
bringing to naught the hopes of fond fathers,
and paving the way for paralysis and general
idiocy.

The evil itself can scarcely be exaggerated,
especially as regards ventilation. There is
probably not a well-ventilated school-house in
the country. I have been in many, and I do
not recollect one that was not repulsive with

foul air. Enter the main hall during the morning exercises, and you may be sufficiently comfortable; but go into a recitation-room during the latter half of the recitation hours and you are actually smitten by the noisome atmosphere. You instinctively breathe shortly to avoid inhaling it. In this filthy bath the delicate lungs of delicate children are immersed and soaked and steeped, hour after hour, for days and months and years, till the nastiness is well incorporated into blood and brain and heart.

And the parents do not care. The fault is wholly and solely with them. The teachers do every thing they can do to mitigate the evil. They open the ventilators; they open the windows, as far as draughts are permissible. At the close of each recitation they give the rooms as complete an airing as possible. It is the parents who build schoolhouses and put their children into them. It is the parents who cram their children's lungs with the same old, used-up, spoiled air over and over again. They do not object to it. They hear talk and make talk about fresh air, but they do not supply fresh air. They would just as soon their children would breathe the foul as the fresh. If they wanted the pure air they would have it. They do not wash their children's faces in dirty water; and clean air is more accessible than clean water. As they do not use it, the inference is that they do not want it.

So of hours and terms and tasks—they all emanate from the parent. The school session is six hours long, when it should be no more than five; but not only is the teacher not responsible for this, but let him advocate earnestly a reduction to five hours, and parents would say he did it for the sake of shirking the hour's work himself. They would think they were not getting their money's worth if school closed at four instead of five, or two instead of three. We want our children in the

school-room six hours. When they are at school
we feel that they are safe. We do not mind
what they are breathing, but we know they are
not roaming the street; they are not drowning
or fighting or running after a circus. They
are taken care of. If you dismiss school at
four, our duration of mental ease is shortened
by an hour—and shall you indolent and easy-
placed teachers have only five hours of work,
while fathers and mothers bear the burden
and heat of a never-ending day?

The course of studies is possibly a little
more under the control of the teacher, but
only a very little. So many years are given
to the primary, so many to the grammar, so
many to the high school. So many studies
the father wishes his son to prosecute. The
subdivision is as rigid as mathematics. The
teacher is powerless. The parent is powerful.
He can take out lessons or put in years. He
can make his high-school course five years
long instead of four, or he can dismiss a lan-

guage or a science from the course. If he do not choose to do it, it is not the teacher's place to do it. Let the teacher attempt it, and he immediately lays himself open to the allegation of desiring to diminish his own work. It is his part to teach what he is appointed to teach, and if he paralyze the children's brains it is no affair of his. He was put there to paralyze them. That is the way he earns his salary. When the farmer sends his grain to mill, the natural inference is that he wants it ground.

It is comfortable to see people uncomfortable in this matter; but it is marvelous to see them angry with any one but themselves.

We religious folk inveigh earnestly against the children's balls and parties in which you of the world indulge; we go to the great hotels and see the little children decked in elaborate finery, and dancing and prancing through the vast rooms before gazing crowds at hours when they ought to be fast asleep in their

L

beds, and, thank Heaven, we mean to keep our
little ones in the sheltered ways of home!

But what objectionable feature of children's
balls was wanting in the series of Pilgrim Memorial festivities not long ago held in Tremont
Temple, Boston? Late hours, fine clothes, gazing crowds, intense excitement, all were there;
and the mothers were not there in a position
to exercise constant care over the wild little
creatures. When I alighted before the door,
out almost upon the sidewalk rushed a little
lady whom I knew to meet me, out into the
midst of the crowd, out into the cold, dark
night — a tiny thing scarcely ten years old,
in flimsy white gown and thin slippers, un-
shawled, bare-headed, unattended except by a
girl of her own age. Half crazy with excitement, the little chits were curveting from
room to room, breathless and eager, unable to
be quiet, their nearest approach to standing
still a nervous hopping and skipping. Presently they were marshaled, and indeed it

was a pretty sight! They fluttered into their
places, tier above tier of white-robed girls rising before us like a bank of lilies; and over
against them the contrasting shadow of sober-
hued boys; and behind, and far above all, an
arched throne occupied by a single little girl,
who, I suppose, represented Liberty, or some
such virtuous abstraction, and who kept one in
constant fear that she would drop asleep and
fall off. Then they sang, and their fresh young
voices thrilled out on the air, and filled the
great hall with melody. They rose, and it
was like the bursting of a bud into broad
white blossom. They waved suddenly their
hidden flags, and the lily bank was alive with
color. Faith, Hope, and Charity, Justice and
Peace, and all the United States, grouped
themselves in their appointed places, and sang
their appointed songs; and so the Pilgrims
were memorialized.

And there were evening concerts and mat-
inees, and for these I do not know how many

rehearsals. A large number of the children were from neighboring towns, and could scarcely have reached home before eleven o'clock. If they were like one little lady, they were not asleep before twelve; and school began next day at nine, as usual. And was it for this, O God, beneath thy guiding hand, our exiled fathers crossed the sea?

Yet people who would on no account send their children to dancing-school let them out to these concerts; and religious papers, that are the first to condemn the frivolities of fashionable mammas, were the first to denounce the Boston public for not filling the Temple to witness this sacrifice of the lambs.

If it were not too serious, it would be grotesque. When "the fashionable mother" takes her little one to the ball-room, and sets her spinning, she honestly gives her of her best. She starts her in the life which she herself most values, for the prizes which herself holds highest. But we Pilgrims profess to scout all that. We deprecate the show, the admiration, the absorption, as the worst things for our children. Yet here we are deliberately bringing it all upon them. We are farming out their youth, their innocence, their fresh, winsome beauty, for paper currency—children fifty cents, reserved seats one dollar. Is not that worse than the fashionable mother? She, at least, does not sell the gift of God for money. If it is right to keep children up till midnight, to show them off before promiscuous assemblies, to set them on fire with excitement, what difference does it make whether we use their toes or their tongues? What difference does it make whether it is in the Tremont Temple or in the Ocean House parlors? If it is right, let us say no more about it. If it is wrong, does the building of a Congregational house with the proceeds make it right? We may have been mistaken hitherto in our abjurations and adjurations; but if we were not, the adoption of such a mode of church-building is very much like laying the foundations of Jericho in the blood of our first-born.

If, when these little goddesses of Liberty and Hope and Charity grow to woman's estate, they choose to go upon the stage in dresses as thin and short as they wore at this Pilgrim opera, and sing drinking-songs instead of greeting-songs, and enact the "Bohemian Girl" instead of the United States, their fathers and mothers may not be able to hinder them. But to thrust them upon the stage in their tender years—to train them for public performances, and feed them with public applause—is a thing which nobody but their parents can do, and for which their parents, aided and abetted, but not governed, by the religious press, are alone responsible.

I do not believe that one child in ten thousand is injured by too close attention to his studies. The injury comes simply from dissipation; from dissipation not connected with but hostile to his studies; not suggested but discountenanced by the teachers, and permitted by the parents. If children sleep and eat and breathe and play rightly, taking their books home from school will not hurt them. If they do not, leaving the books at school will not help them. A girl is no more harmed by studying her multiplication-table till nine than she is by singing in a public concert-room for charity till eleven.

One who was reproached with attempting to forward a benevolent object by turning the children into beggars as well as public performers, replied, in substance, " We do nothing of the sort; we simply urge the children to give us their own earnings, and such small contributions as they may solicit from their parents and casual visitors."

If there were no begging but street begging, the charge is disproved; but begging in the house is far worse than begging out of it. The little, shivering, hungry, forlorn wretch who timidly holds out his hat at the street crossings, or the still more common little wretch who has added to his poverty hypocrisy, who follows you into the railroad station, and in an exaggerated whine asks you for money to buy a loaf of bread for his sick mother—these have the dire and awful excuse of hunger. Famine is a foe to delicacy, and rags chill self-respect to death. But why should we turn to, and with malice aforethought, for a far-off and perhaps shadowy good, destroy the modesty and blunt the sense of propriety of our own little, plump, rosy, healthy lads and lasses? The money can by no means do good enough to atone for the harm done to the child by enjoining or permitting a child to ask money of his father's visitors, or of any outside person, for any purpose whatever. There is bluntness enough in our social relations, Heaven knows. We lift our standard of duty over other people's heads, dictate to them their benevolence, their relig-

ion, and the size of their families; but the
next generation will surpass us in our imperti-
nence if we thus train them up to it from
their tender years. What is improper in
grown people is grotesquely improper in children. And it is always improper and impertinent for one person to urge another to bestow
in charity. If a case of destitution be brought
to the knowledge of one man, he may lay it
before others, and present any plan for assist-
ance that he may have formed; but that is all.
He is not to solicit alms. When persons know
the suffering, the matter lies in their hands
alone. For what they do or do not they alone
are responsible. Still less for large organized
charities should men solicit contributions. Let
them give what publicity they choose to their
objects and methods; let ministers preach sermons explanatory and exhortatory if they will;
but let all the rest be left to the action of individuals. For convenience an agent may be
appointed to receive what people have to be-

stow; but the man who comes to my house
and urges me to give fifty dollars, or five dollars, or fifty cents, to any body or any thing,
is impertinent, and if I had not better manners
than he I should tell him so.   Happily the art
of printing has been invented for the purpose
of giving us a chance to say behind people's
backs what we will not say to their faces.   To
put the facts on the lowest ground, he does not
know what is my income nor what are my
expenses, and he has, therefore, no possible
means of knowing what I am able to give, or
whether I can give any thing.   Moreover, I
may not have faith in his aims, his society, or
himself; but, of course, I do not wish to tell
him so, though, if he annoy me overmuch,
there is danger that I shall, and with some
heat.   But worse than this, by the very act of
urging me to charity, he becomes offensive.
He puts himself on a plane above me; he assumes that I will not do what I ought unless
he, with his superior goodness, urge me to it

—which may all be true, but a truth which it is not his province to preach.

But what will our charities come to, cry the benevolent, if we are to be so squeamish? What shall we come to if we are not so squeamish is quite as important a question. If the heathen Chinee can not become Christian without Christians becoming busybodies in other men's matters, why, Christianity has two sides. If Christians do not care enough about their Gospel and their fellows to send the one to the other, the true way is to make them better Christians, not work upon their pride or their vanity, and make them send the Gospel anyhow. Let not your left hand know what your right hand doeth, says Christ, as clear as crystal; and we obey his injunction by sending around a subscription-paper with all the names and gifts in black and white— " John Doe, twenty dollars; Richard Roe, fifteen dollars" — and the excuse is that you would not get half as much any other way;

that is, Christians will not give for love half as much as they will give for shame or show. If this were so, would it not be well to leave the heathen Chinee, and turn our guns upon ourselves?

We greatly need more delicacy, more knowledge of limitations, more sense of propriety, more respect for the rights and the individuality of others. If we wish to build a memorial hall, and send an agent around with a subscription-paper, his object ought not to be to make as many people give as much as possible, but, primarily, to save people the trouble of carrying their contributions to head-quarters; and, secondarily, to spare them any possible pain or embarrassment in not making a contribution. The best agent is not the one who collects the most money, but the one who leaves in the hearts of those he has visited the strongest conviction that benevolence is gentle, considerate, courteous. When benevolence attempts to pry into your affairs, or to override your decisions, or to take advantage of your position, or in any way to dictate your course, you feel inclined to close your purse-strings and open your door.

That little children should not only be permitted but instructed to levy contributions on their parents' visitors—who can not do so ungracious a thing as to refuse, no matter what their sentiments or opinions may be—shows a marvelous misunderstanding or perversion of the laws of politeness and hospitality, and a marvelous ignorance of or indifference to the delicacy of a child's nature.

VIII.

DISCIPLINING CHILDREN.

My friend Heraclitus, lover of children, is much concerned in mind at the disappearance of discipline from the American nursery. He sees in the child-world precocity, fun, slang, swearing, natural naughtiness, little goodness but that resulting from natural impulses, docile papas and mammas, who either rule by love or let ruling alone altogether. He laments exceedingly that Miss Edgeworth is out of date, and avers that she would turn pale at our notions of instruction if she were not, chiefly, it appears, because "nobody is unpleasantly disciplined;" and he mournfully predicts as the result of our "false coddling" that the poor little coddled boy will rest satisfied with his slipshod good-nature and his bad-breeding, and will not care a fig for such superfluities as discipline, endurance, modesty, and reverence.

To illustrate his position and prove his assertions, my friend brings forward a juvenile story wherein a little girl-visitor insists on having her own question answered before she will answer a question put to her, to the amusement of her lady-hostess. This Heraclitus considers to be a lesson in those bad manners so notorious in American children. But is it a lesson in bad manners to children? Is it not rather a lesson in good manners to the children's mothers? What would you have? The little girl was not the lady's child, but a visitor. Was it a case where "discipline" could be properly applied? Whoever studies, with love and sympathy, the ways of children, knows that Dr. Franklin and all the forefathers were not more jealous of their rights, more indignant at usurped authority, than are children in the nursery. No child of ordinary sense and spirit but would resent discipline or reproof administered by any one but its legal rulers. And the children are right, notorious bad manners though it be. The rules of polite society apply to children just as radically as to adults. Grown people are often in society called upon to suppress their own feelings, sometimes to sacrifice their own tastes, sometimes to soften the expression of their own principles, out of regard to the exigencies of politeness and peace. It is just as true in our intercourse with children. You are no more required to tell a child-guest what you think of him, what is wrong or impolite in his behavior, than you are required to tell an adult guest. A child's feelings are as sensitive as a man's, and his power of self-defense far weaker. He will gradually learn of himself to correct his own impoliteness, but the interference of a foreign hand may inflict a life-long wound. It is a mistake to suppose that every person is under bonds immediately to correct every fault in every child he sees. Many faults he will amend of his own accord, out of pride and love and self-respect. Leave him alone. There is no surer way to build up a child's self · respect than to pay him your own; there is no better way to teach him good manners than to practice good manners toward him.

If Heraclitus, lover of children, practice his own principles, he is an object for commiseration. When he sits at the tables of his friends, and reproves Mary for soiling the table-cloth, and sends Fred into a corner for thumping Harry, and rebukes Susy because her hair is not tidy, and flogs Samuel for insubordination, let no politeness of his friends deceive him into thinking himself a welcome guest. Parents may hold the reins of power exceeding loosely, but they have a strong prejudice against suffering any outside hand to usurp their hold; and as for the little ill-bred imps themselves, I greatly fear they would give

M

Heraclitus but a moral crucifixion in return for his excellent " discipline."

I go further, and say that even if the lady had been the child's mother, it is not at all certain that she did not do the wisest thing. We lay it to the necessity of breaking a child's will. Why need a child's will be broken? He will have use for it all. The difference between strength of will and weakness of will is often the difference between efficiency and inefficiency. Train a child to self-control, so that his will may be his strong point, but do not break his will. We read heart-rending accounts of prolonged struggles between a baby and its father, resulting, after hours and sometimes days of mutual agony, in parental victory—of course! It would not be wise to say that this is always unwise. There may be occasions when willfulness and obstinacy and wrong must be directly met and mastered, but, as a general rule, such issues are to be avoided. It is not

a fair fight. The little one is so ignorant, so
helpless, so bewildered! The father is strong
and well equipped. *Noblesse oblige.* Let the
superior wisdom be used in turning aside an-
tagonism rather than in overcoming it. Half
the time the disobedience was originally innocent. It was the expression merely of a temporary mood, a half-unconscious physical dis-
inclination, the mere intentness of a mind
strongly and singly set on its own aims, and
wholly free from evil intent and moral turpi-
tude. But the parental insistence develops the
antagonistic determination, and so raises the
devil which it subsequently prides itself on cast-
ing out. In the case under notice, the little girl
had probably no spite, no mischief, no willfulness even, in her heart. All her little soul was
absorbed in her own thought. If there were
willfulness, it was of a very innocent sort,
scarcely to be distinguished from playfulness;
and it is far more dignified for a mature and
cultivated mind to yield lovingly and play-

fully to the impetuousness of the little savage than to overshadow it with ponderosity, and magnify it into a case of gravity and discipline. As between obedience and disobedience there is no choice; it is a misfortune to a child—though not a fatal one—not to be so trained that obedience is natural and instinctive. Parental law is to him what natural and civil law are to the adult. The parent may fail to enforce law, but God and society are stern. If one be not taught to bear the yoke in his youth, it will be a heavy burden to his manhood; for bear the yoke he must. If he do not control himself, society will control him, bitterly; and the longer self-control is delayed, the harder it is to learn. Moreover, a child is as much happier as he is stronger for being subject to, held up by, reasonable law. None are so wretched as he who is given over to be preyed upon by his own moods and passions. But the relation between parent and child is not so inelastic as to involve nothing

else than obedience and disobedience. There
is ample room for the play of freedom and
mirth and badinage. Very small children understand the difference between literal and
figurative statements, between real and mock
commands, between assumed and actual stern-
ness. Long before Jaime has stepped out of
tucks and embroidery, before his little feet
have wholly mastered the secret of steering
and steadiness, he perfectly comprehends that
when you say, "Jaime, I will eat you up!"
it is no cannibal's threat, and he enters into
the spirit of it with well feigned distress, and
much shielding of dimpling cheeks with dimpled hands, and brilliant evolutions of flight
and pursuit. While essential obedience should
be secured, wide margin should be granted for
the nourishment and expansion of a child's
own individuality, for his peculiar mental action, and for the cultivation and gratification
of his tastes. This may lapse into weak and
vicious indulgence, but even this is no worse

than arrogant and tyrannical exercise of power, which takes no cognizance of a child's separate selfhood, but alike in great things and
in small makes itself first, and exacts from
the child only prompt and perfect submission.
The wise parent is as far removed from the
one extreme as from the other. Neither license nor slavery; but liberty is as good for
the child as for his parents. And if this liberty
bring about that rectitude of the natural impulses by which Heraclitus sets so small store,
and diminish the necessity for that "unpleas-
ant discipline" by which he sets so great store,
is it indeed a consummation devoutly to be
deprecated? I can not see why it is more
virtuous to be obliged to tie your hands in order to keep from stealing than it is not to
want to steal. It seems to me that a family
or a national administration is more success-
ful if it diminish the inclination to wrong-
doing than if it punish wrong-doing. He who
makes obedience and deference "natural im-

pulses" is a better disciplinarian than he who flogs for disobedience and impoliteness.

My friend is also moved with disgust at the lack of heroism displayed in juvenile management. He evidently thinks we are training a race of women who will rival that princess whose royal birth was proved by the fact that three peas placed under the twenty piled-up mattresses upon which she was lying had bruised her black and blue before morning. He objects to such a sentiment as that pain is too dreadful to be accepted when it can be avoided, because it tends to depreciate courage. If parents, unwilling to use mere authority to gain a child's consent to a dreaded but necessary surgical operation, and having vainly exhausted reasoning to prove its necessity, at length offer some valued boon, some long-coveted possession, he looks upon it as outrageous bribery. But does Heraclitus mean that pain is to be accepted when it can be avoided ? That is not courage ; it is folly, or, at the best, insensibility. If a man is more afraid of ether than he is of the forceps, he may well reject ether, but he may not call it courage. I suppose almost any one who had strength of nerve, strength of muscle, and a jackknife could extract an effete tooth if you would give him time enough. Yet the suffering owner would probably go to the skilled dentist who could disembarrass him most swiftly and deftly of the offending member. And he is no coward for preferring to be relieved by a master rather than extricated by a clod-hopper. Neither is he a coward for going still further, and annihilating all consciousness of pain. To escape necessary suffering is as wise as to bear with fortitude inevitable suffering is heroic. But to make a little girl endure pain rather than endure a little anxiety or take a little trouble yourself, is, like swearing, "neither brave, polite, nor wise."

It would be admirable if children could be made always to listen to reason. Yet reasoning is sometimes, even among grown people, vainly exhausted. Is it therefore incredible and monstrous that children should occasionally be impervious to its appeals? Men are most logically incarcerated and executed, but if they had the power they would, with the utmost sophistry, escape. The gift which a fond father offers his daughter to induce her to submit consentingly to a dreaded but necessary operation, rather than to force her by mere authority to submit, may or may not be wise, but to call it "outrageous bribery" is to use words without knowledge—is to speak as the foolish women speak in those conventions which Heraclitus is the first to discountenance, not to say ridicule. If Heraclitus does not like the way in which parents manage their children, it is not necessary that he should give a reason for his disapprobation. He may stand with folded arms and "make faces" at them from his own "natural impulses" if it seem good to him, but if he insists upon pro-

ducing reasons, and furnishes no better than
these, let him not hope to cause any great diminution of parental injudiciousness and indulgence.

He thinks that the bad manners of American children are notorious, and lays a large
part of it to the neglect of Miss Edgeworth
and the going astray after false gods. We
have heard so much of these bad manners that
it may be presumptuous to question our emi-
nence in ill-breeding. Still, a too emphatic
and prolonged crimination has a tendency to
defeat its end and instigate recrimination.
What may be the manner of Irish children I
have small means of knowing. They at least
have had the advantage of the instruction
and example of the excellent Miss Edgeworth,
whom we highly and justly extol. Nevertheless Miss Edgeworth's own brother grew up,
we are told, with every virtue except those
which belong to civilization. He hated books,
hated government of every sort, and finally

ran off to sea. If Miss Edgeworth's theories
of juvenile management were framed from
what she saw, the result is not so encouraging
that we need copy it. If they were the natural rebound from what she saw, it is hardly
fair to extol Irish at the expense of American
children.

My personal knowledge of English children
is equally limited ; but so far as we can judge
from popular literature, from the story-tellers
and the caricaturists, it would seem that the
children and youth of England are not better
bred than those of America. I think American society would be ransacked in vain for
such fierce and violent vulgarity as is found in
the pages of popular novelists like Thackeray
and Miss Austen. I am very sure that no son
of any American family prominent in literary
or social life would think it good manners to
sit on the supper-table when attending a party
at a friend's house, though a son of a very high
family in England did not consider it an im-

proper mark of respect or disrespect for his host, as I am assured by eye-witnesses. American discipline may be at a low ebb, but if an American boy's *penchant* for sitting on supper-tables had not been broken up by his parents before he was five years old, the young man's ability to do so would be speedily destroyed by the first gentleman at whose table he should attempt it.

I should be sorry to say any thing that might aid and abet our idle, lax, and worthless American fathers and mothers. But it is an indisputable fact that children do take an immense deal of spoiling without permanent injury if there is good stock in them. Nature seems to think more of substance than training, for she gives children not when people are wisest, but when they are freshest and strongest. It is delightful to see children always behaving with perfect propriety and politeness ; but if they kick and cuff and scream and grab, all is not lost. There is a certain

governor whom not having seen I love, because
he sends word to his son that his grandson is
the best little fellow in the world if you do
not thwart him, and always obedient if you
will only not hurry him about it. The Baby
in Breeches was standing by my chair, and I
clandestinely snatched a kiss, whereupon up
flew his chubby hand and gave me a smart
slap on the cheek. It was in my heart to re-
tort with a thump, but I refrained, and by and
by, when I whispered, "Why did you strike
me?" he answered, innocently, "Because you
stole a kiss." Innocent as an angel, for it was
pure frolic, and no malice or rudeness at all.
But we expect to take liberties with children,
and then have them perfectly wise and aware
of the exact degree of respect to be observed
toward ourselves.

Oh, careful and mistrusting parent, let no
Heraclitus without or within destroy your peace
of mind. It is not only the good and gentle,
but also the froward child, who is going to

give you credit by and by : the wild and wayward, the turbulent and uproarious little miscreant whom you can not manage, who seems
to be beyond your control—perhaps he *is* beyond your control.   In fact, all children are
beyond parental control.   They are separate
and independent human beings, with tastes
and tendencies and tempers as distinct as if
they were a hundred years old.   You feel that
wise training is of the utmost importance, and
so it is ; but if you lack wisdom, love is often
wiser than wisdom.   This, at least, is sure : the
most impressive and effective parental training is in the parent himself.   The father and
mother can do nothing worse for their child
than to be themselves false and fretful and
fault-finding ; they can do nothing better for
him than to be themselves upright, frank, generous, large-hearted, respected, and honored.
No instruction is so thorough as the constant
and unconscious instruction conveyed when
the parents are all that they wish their chil-

dren to become, and this instruction they have always under their own control. The little ones, if they are of an enterprising turn, will often tread a zigzag path ; but it is almost certain to tend constantly upward, and bring them presently into the table-lands of high thought and honorable words and courtliness, and the desire of fame and love of truth, and all that makes a man—or a woman !

IX.

THE WARDS OF THE NATION.

THE noble savage of the Southwest is not a pleasant person to fall in with except in novels. He is not only fierce and cruel and treacherous, all of which he might be without forfeiting his niche in romance, but, not to put too fine a point on it, he is a very lazy, a very dirty, a very disgusting noble savage. Therefore he is not a good character to work up into novels until he is translated into the romance language. It is not, alas! impossible to construct a temporary hero out of an assassin; but all the unities and all the proprieties rise up in revolt against a hero who makes his toilet by greasing himself from head to foot; whose sole garment is a coarse cotton cloth, perpetually guiltless of the laundry; who is too lazy even to hunt, but depends for his living on what he can steal from his industrious and ambitious white neighbor; who lounges in idleness while his women, old and young alike, toil in his thankless service; and who, by his indolence and his general and total depravity, has become a squalid, emaciated, and loathsome horror.

In pursuit of their natural avocation these noble savages, our brethren of the Apaches, Kioways, and other tribes, have a way of pouncing upon our frontier settlements, slaying the men, capturing the women and children, and bearing them away to a life more horrible than all the imaginations of death.

Colonel Leavenworth, son of the man whose name has become a part of the history and geography of Kansas, acting under orders from our government, was wont occasionally to descend upon these outlying tribes to rescue, peaceably if he could, forcibly if he must, such captives as might have fallen into their clutches. A little while ago he made such a

N

descent, and succeeded in ransoming from the mouth of hell a wretched company of women and children.

Among these were two little girls, apparently of three and five years of age, whom none of the captives claimed, whose name no one knew, whose origin no one could conjecture. Two little waifs tossed up by a cruel sea upon an unknown shore—two little pitiful children, they stood before the pitying man, with pale, wistful faces, with matted hair, with scanty clothing, silent, sad-eyed, bereft, overborne by a weight of woe too heavy for them to comprehend. Torn from the rude, hardy, yet civilized frontier life, thrust at tender age into the unfathomable depths of brutal barbarism, their little souls seemed already to have sunk into the nether darkness. Their own names had faded from their memory. But it was Anglo-Saxon blood in their veins; and when the fresh, pure air breathed over it, slowly it began to run red and bright once more. Won by friendly words and much gentle urgency, light faintly broke upon their darkened memories; and to persistent questioning, in sorrowful, fragmentary sentences, with childish, tragic, uncomprehending simplicity, their mournful history unfolded itself. They remembered father and mother. The Indians came. They saw the Indians cut their father's hair off. The Indians shot their mother. Uncle Jim was on horseback. Uncle Jim had the baby. The Indians shot Uncle Jim. Baby fell down. Indians killed the baby on the ground. Such was the story of their brief life—a story told with a shrinking reluctance, with a shuddering awe that spoke all too vividly of the horror engraven upon their consciousness. According to the Indian custom, one of these children had already been adopted by a squaw whose own child was dead. Colonel Leavenworth succeeded in buying them, and started on his journey northward. The wily but noble savage followed and stole them both back again.

The Colonel returned, and grimly enough
made a second bargain and paid a second ran-
som.   A characteristic trait of these stalwart
sons of the forest is to kill rather than release
their captives.   Having received their money
a second time, they dispatched the children in
charge of a squaw to Colonel Leavenworth.
Crossing the Washita River on horseback, this
well-meaning matron chanced, in course of
conversation, to slip the oldest child into the
water; but a young squaw behind, more
friendly or more far-seeing, plunged into the
river, rescued the gasping girl, and placed her
safely in the hands of Colonel Leavenworth.
In the careful guardianship of the Colonel
and his family, the little creatures made the
long journey back to the East, and to the civilization which their unknown ancestors had
left unknown years before.   No home awaited
them—no kindred knew them.   Cut off from
all the world, isolated by a strange and dreadful fate, they belonged to the nation.   Not of

charity, but in strict justice, the country that should have protected the parents adopted the children. The Government—the broad, unseen, mighty power that guards all greatness, yet reckons nothing too weak for its cherishing—bent like a god, and took them in. In an orphan home, under the very shadows of that central dome which springs aloft beautiful as a dream of the heavens above, and strong as the solid earth beneath, close to the great sheltering heart of the nation, the tired feet were stayed, the little wanderers found rest. Nameless, the nation gave them a name; and what so fitting as his whose heart softened with unutterable tenderness to the sorrows of the helpless and lowly? So, with rare delicacy, the little ones were endued with the name of the Good President; and now, among the somewhat dry, and sometimes dreary records of the "Forty-first Congress, Second Session," you shall read, with a thrill which all the formal phraseology can not repress:

"*Whereas*, The Kioway Indians, on or about the fifth day of January, eighteen hundred and sixty-eight, captured, in Cook County, in the State of Texas, two female children, whose family name is unknown, aged about three and five years, after having murdered the parents and all the known relatives of said children ; *and whereas* said children have recently been recovered from said Indians, and are now in the care of J. H. Leavenworth, and are without any means of support ;

"*Therefore, be it resolved, by the Senate and House of Representatives of the United States of America, in Congress assembled,* That the Secretary of the Interior is hereby directed to reserve, from any annuities due, or to become due, to said Kioway Indians, the sum of two thousand five hundred dollars for each of said children, and cause the same to be placed to their credit on the books of the Treasury of the United States, to bear interest at the rate of five per centum per annum, and use, from time to time, the income from the same in such manner as he may deem expedient for their maintenance, education, and support, during their lifetime, until they attain the age of twenty-one years, when the principal shall be paid them ; and the elder of said children shall be hereafter known as Helen Lincoln, and the younger as Heloise Lincoln."

Curiosity, and perhaps some better motive, led me to visit these friendless little orphans, now royally befriended. A pleasant-faced,

motherly woman had them in charge, and it
was easy to see that they could scarcely have
fallen into better hands. It was a very motherly gratification that smiled in her face at the
announcement that Congress had passed the
bill providing for their support. They came
in, hand-in-hand, two tiny creatures, quaint
and demure in dress and demeanor. Every
question they answered with promptness and
decision, but without spontaneity. No encouragement could bring out any childish prattle,
or cause any thing but a momentary up-look
to the downcast eyes. Yet the matron said
that among children they would play and
chatter with the rest, though with adults they
maintained this unbroken reserve, which no
association had enabled them to throw off.
To Colonel Leavenworth, with whom they had
lived and traveled, to her, as well as to strangers, they were invariably silent, unless questioned, and then they answered in fewest
words. The habits and ways which they had
contracted among the Indians were at first very

troublesome. They had little notion of the use or abuse of clothes, and refused many ordinary articles of food; but they constantly improved, and had already learned not only to read and write a little, but to wear clothes, which is a good deal harder. They spoke with great reluctance of their life among the Indians, answering in monosyllables when possible. I thought I saw a reminiscence of suffering and terror in a certain veiled and filmy look of the eye; but perhaps it is only nature's defense against the too strong light of outdoor life; and there seemed something of Indian undemonstrativeness in the passivity with which they met all advances. Yet when, fearing to embarrass the child, I would have let go the hand I was holding, I noticed that the little fingers curled back into mine as if the touch were pleasant.

I am sure that all fatherly and motherly hearts will warm toward these fatherless and motherless, and their angels do always behold the face of our Father which is in heaven.

X.

SEPARATION.

ONE is often tempted to echo that modest remark of a certain wise man that, if he had been present at the creation of the world, he. thought he should have been able to give its Maker a few suggestions. There *are* a few things, in fact a good many things, which one would like to have altered, and which might apparently just as well have been made differ ent in the beginning. And yet, on the whole, there is a wonderful adaptation in things as they are. To make much improvement, you must change so many cases that, before you know it, you will find you have projected a new world.

Sometimes one is tempted to think that, if the family could not be somehow constituted to hold together, we might as well not have

had mankind set in families. The father and
mother make their little home. The children
laugh and cry, and work and play; they have
mumps and measles and " teething " and scar-
latina; they have little tiffs with each other;
they are bumped and bruised; they knock out
their teeth, and set their clothes on fire, and
come home at irregular intervals, with a black
eye or a broken arm. So, under constant
watching, with many retrogressions and a thousand hair-breadth escapes, they wind along the
tortuous path of right living, and presently the
oldest child has arrived at the comparative
maturity of — let us say thirteen years. He
takes an interest in raw but real science—if it
is very raw—in mechanics, in politics. The
amount of information he has acquired on all
subjects is astonishing. He has penetrated
machine - shops, mounted locomotives, trotted
after soldiers, made love to sailors, and few
things in the heavens above, or the earth beneath, or the waters under the earth, have es-

caped his observation. Now, at thirteen, he
begins to consolidate, and you would say his
father and mother might have some good of
him. Not that they have not had good of
him before, prattling, bumping, and bruising
through his infancy and early boyhood; but
it was a comfort largely compounded with
care. It was a delight in bounding health and
beauty, and grace and promise, always under-
laid with a fearful consciousness that, when
the beauty and grace was not snugly tucked
up in bed, it might be sliding down the third-
story baluster, or bestriding the ridge-pole of
the barn, at the imminent risk of its beautiful
and graceful neck. Only now, when baluster
and ridge-pole have lost their irresistible first
charm, and top and kite and ball are not para-
mount objects of interest—now, when the cau-
cus and concert and play begin to loom up,
and the far-off sun of manhood reddens the
eastern sky—now they can really enjoy him
without misgiving. Do they? Not in the

least. As soon as he ceases to be an hourly care he must go off to school! When he was of no use to any body his parents took him wholly upon themselves; but as soon as he begins to be of the smallest account they have to give him up to the public. No organized tyranny demands him, but just as surely and authoritatively society stretches out its hand and clutches him. His new shirts, his fresh jackets and spotless handkerchiefs are put into his box, and out he goes into the great world for ever and ever. True, he will come back for the vacation, with half his handkerchiefs lost, his jackets out at elbows, and his every-day boots serenely packed atop his pile of shirts; and for several years he will oscillate between home and school; but home for life he will never come again. Home, the eternal resting-place—home, his absorbing and exclusive world—has ceased to be. His childish, instinctive, savage love his parents had; but as soon as he is capable of an intelligent, manly affection, he goes straightway and falls in love with a stranger! It is a consolation to reflect that he is then at the same point whence his father and mother started, and will travel the same round, and see precisely how good it is.

The wonder is that it is pretty good, after all. Dreadful as it may be for parents to give up their child, it would be still more dreadful not to give him up. It is next to impossible for the grown children of a family to stay at home honorably. Life may so adjust itself that this is the best possible arrangement; but usually the sons who have energy, enterprise, character, push out into the world. What good has the mother in her empty house, with one son in China, and one in California, and one in Chicago, and one on the high seas? The foolish mother thinks she has vast treasure still, and conceives immediately a deep and abiding interest in all those places. Instead of dismissing her son from her thought, she takes into her heart at once all the ends of the earth and all the paths of the sea. Not a newspaper scrap from China or California escapes her eye. The scope of her mind has become enlarged through the scope of her affection, and her son's good name in Cathay makes her as proud and happy as if she heard his praise resounding under her own roof-tree.

It is frequent parting that softens the asperity and sweetens the bitterness and mitigates the fierceness of association. Human nature is so sharp and strong and self-willed, that it is a great trial for human beings to live together. The substantial traits of character may be harmonious; but little tastes, slight individualities, opposing tempers, will clash; and even Christian forbearance, generous yielding, kindly courtesy, need the occasional help of absence to keep life permanently sweet. Absence is the great idealizer, and withal, perhaps, the most truthful painter. Your stout, healthy, noisy boy, who teased his sisters, and tossed his pillows, and broke furniture, and tried even his mother's patience, has gone away; and in his silent room you only think how bright and frank and fearless he is—how generous, alert, and eager. The friend and companion whose impatience irritated you, whose indecision annoyed you, whose impromptitude exasperated you, has crossed the seas, and you remember only how truthful he was, how loyal, how devoted, how unselfish.

It is parting, indeed, that plows great furrows in the heart, but it keeps the soil mellow and open, receptive and fertile. Made as we are, we should grow, without it, too hard, exacting, unresponsive, unforgiving. With the pain of parting always near, with the shadow of one parting never far, it is easy to repress the hasty word, to discern the sunny side, to veil the weakness with charity, and nourish the strength with love. The heart grows soft and tender and considerate, self fades and selfishness dies, and the whole being goes out in eager desire to succor and bless its beloved.

Alas! for the deepening shadows of the one parting.

On a pleasant summer morning I was walking up the village street. Far ahead of me, three little children were playing in the road. A venerable horse was sauntering slowly along, cropping the rich grass by the wayside. As he passed the children, they left their play and gave chase, in dangerous proximity to his heels. By the time I came up they had resumed their sport, and were fashioning wonderful hills and lakes and ranges of mountains out of the clean, fine, deep, delicious dust for such case made and provided from the foundation of the world. One little lad and lass were old friends of mine. The third I had never seen; but I was confident he was the son of an old friend, and, taking a liberty on which I should not venture with an adult, but in which we often indulge where children are concerned, I quite overlooked my acquaintances, and at once accosted the stranger. I was well paid for my bad manners, since, though the young gentleman answered my questions with promptness and civility, his attention was not to be diverted from physical geography, and I could hardly get enough of his interest to secure a satisfactory survey of his face. Presently my old friend, Davy, thought he had been left out in the cold long enough; and, determining to come into notice, he drew himself up and addressed me, with great sonorousness—"How do you do, Mr. John Doe?"

This, of course, effected a diversion; and then I told them how dangerous it was to run so close to the horse's heels.

"Oh," said the little stranger, "he would not hurt *me!* I am a big boy. I am four months older than Davy. I am six years old!"

"He thinks that is every thing!" said Davy, in an undertone of mingled envy and contempt.

"*I* am six and a half!" piped Queen Bess,

O

with the air of one who had reached the height of undisputed supremacy.

And so I left them under the arching elms. The shadows danced over their pretty unconscious heads, the sunlight touched them softly, the music of their chattering voices followed me afar—three dainty little children playing with the dust of the street, all unassoiled.

And now from his distant home come the woeful tidings that the little stranger boy has gone to a more distant home. That curly head lies low. These first winter snows are falling upon his grave.

Only once I saw him, brighter than the sunshine, under the elms; but my heart is heavy for the home bereft of its only child.

Why do the little ones die? Sometimes we can plainly see and admire the wisdom of the divine arrangement. Ignorance and poverty combine to banish wholesome food and pure air and cleanliness and warmth, and the feeble blood fails, and the little sufferer escapes out

of life. That is a lesson easy to understand.
We must bestir ourselves, we say, to dissemi-
nate knowledge of common physical facts, to
enforce sanitary measures. It is Nature's own
teaching severe, but necessary and beneficial.
If people can not learn to be clean in person
and atmosphere, except by the death of their
children, the children must die. Yes; but
by and by our own children sicken—our own
children, who are washed and dressed and fed
and exercised in the fullest light of law and
Gospel. Every thing that is known of hygiene we know. Every thing that can be
done for health and strength we do. In-
door purity and out door play minister to the
child's welfare; and, in spite of all our love
and all our lore, there he lies on his little
bed, with filmy eyes, with parched lips, sick
unto death.

Why is it? Neither parent nor doctor can
tell the cause or the cure of this illness.
There is nothing in the child's training to ac-

count for it. His training, his constitution, account only for health. His parents are strong, his life has been simple. Something wrong has been done; but we know not what. Some unknown law has been violated; but why does God punish us for the violation of an unknown law? Alas! there is grace in the Gospel, but in the law is no room for grace. Revealed religion is merciful, but natural religion demands an eye for an eye and a tooth for a tooth. Paul confidently counted on pardon because he sinned ignorantly; but for physical sins, whether of ignorance, or indolence, or wanton indulgence, or active malice, there is no forgiveness. The little child, innocent, lies on his bed of restlessness and suffering and death—suffering for no sin of his own. The parents, more than innocent, eager to do right, utterly self-sacrificing, watch by their child, helpless, sorrowing, tortured for some unsurmised error or some ancestral wrong.

I have heard it said that every sickness is
intended to be a reminder of sin. In one
sense this is undoubtedly true. If sin is a
violation of divine law, all sickness springs
from sin. God made man upright, but he
hath sought out many diseases. But unconscious violation of law is hardly called sin,
and a large part of sickness springs from an
unconscious violation of law. Neither the
man nor his parents are guilty because he was
born blind. If sickness mean sin in the sufferer or his kin, then health means holiness,
and saints may be judged by as well as in
their bodies.

But these things come, say others, to teach
us trust in God and resignation to the divine
will. But what is the divine will? It is that
children shall be born, and grow up, and die
in ripe old age. It is not the divine will that
brings about the slaughter of the innocents:
it is human weakness cutting athwart the divine will. How can the sickness and death

of a well-born and carefully reared child teach trust in God? What sort of trust does it inculcate? Trust in what sort of a God? A God of inexorable law; a conviction that penalty follows even unwitting transgression, though innocence is crushed and hearts are broken; a terrible misgiving that power is stronger than pity. Ah! I do not think these sorrows teach, but they try man's trust in God. The faith is strong indeed that does not waver then. Job could say, "Though he slay me, yet will I trust in him;" but even he does not say, *Because* he slay me will I trust.

The Divine Being is rich in resources, and has many ways to come at his creatures. Nor does he confine himself to one end in the use of means; but, with the utmost economy, accomplishes many objects by a single stroke. But it seems to me that the very last and least of all the lessons he teaches is resignation. When an unlooked-for calamity happens, the one thing we ought not to do is to be resigned to it. We ought to be resigned to that system of things under which it happens, because it is the divine system. Hard and heavy as the blow may fall on us, we may still trust that God is good and kind, though he seem pitiless, and would not have let us suffer if he could have helped it. But his plans are, on the whole, the best that could be devised, and there is no way but this to bring us to a knowledge of his truth. But to fold our hands in passive resignation is to make the suffering of none effect. "Nature is lavish," says the father of six dead and two living children. "A thousand blossoms overspread the tree, and but few grow into fruit. God's will be done." Very true. But if the farmer found that three fourths of his calves, lambs, pigs, chickens, died every spring, would he talk of resignation? On the contrary, he would take the most active measures to discover the cause of the fatality; and, if he could not discover it, he would speedily give up farming. Are not children of more value than many calves? Is it reasonable to suppose that it is the divine will that lambs should live, but that the far more elaborate, more costly, more precious human infant, made in the very image of God, should perish? Yet people whom a fatality in the barnyard would incite to persistent investigation and consultation and thought and experiment will see child after child die, and never suspect that they are called upon for any thing but resignation.

Fortunately for us, God is so abundant, not only in loving kindness, but in modes of expressing it, that, though we miss the main lesson, we learn many subordinate ones. A thousand parents suffer and nothing seems to come of it. But by and by rises a man who has eyes to see. He piles fact upon fact, deduces therefrom a law, and the world is wiser for his living, and the children of the future have

one more chance for life. But meanwhile
the thousand parents who had no thought of
cause and effect, who see God only in church-
ly relations, in infinite leisure, in the remote
heavens, and never as a God close at hand in
the ceaseless activity of every-day life, they,
too, have drawn a little nearer to him—a little
nearer by sorrow to all the sorrowful. They
have grown finer through the ministry of pain;
they have become detached from the narrow
by the mystery of the wider life. So blindly
we feel after God, and find him in the skies,
though we miss him where he stands, not far
from every one of us.

And still, blindly groping, may we not find
another solace?

It was the picture of a man twenty-two
years old. The youthful face was fair, fresh,
guileless as a child's, yet strong and steadfast,
with all the promise of manhood. Looking at
the full, firm outlines, at the pure and vivid
coloring, at the expression, singularly frank,

simple, and engaging, one found himself involuntarily saying, "Strength and beauty are in his sanctuary."

It was the face of a young man smitten down in his opening manhood to a sudden and cruel death. No disease mastered him, no imprudence or ignorance of his own overtook him, no sacred cause demanded the sacrifice of his young years. But an incredible and most guilty carelessness on the part of another sped the swift bullet, and in a moment, in the twinkling of an eye, before love could even look upon him, he was torn away from sweet life. All the pleasure and the pains lavished on his two-and-twenty years— mother's woe and mother's love, the culture of school and home, paternal pride and trust, social joys, memories and hopes of fireside happiness—all crushed beneath one bitter blow, all buried in one untimely grave.

Opposite hangs another picture. It is the face of a man one hundred and two years old.

The features are sharp, the eyes sunken, and with a sort of wistful, eager, submissive sadness, as of eyes that have " looked in vain." The whole face is plowed with furrows, the form is shrunken, thin, and bent. It is a hundred and two years old.

And I look back upon the sunny, sweet face opposite, immortal in its youth, and I can not ask which is the better fate? Instinctively I feel through all my shuddering soul that life may be more tragic than death.

It is true—it is terribly, hopelessly true—that

> "Not all the preaching since Adam
> Can make death other than death."

The hearthstone is cold every night, and the table newly vacant each morning, and the silence freshly and forever vital with loss, while we long with unspeakable longing and ceaseless pain, not for the conclusions of philosophy, not—ah! Heaven be kind!—not for the consolations of religion; but for the very face which we shall never see, for the ringing, merry, happy voice which through all the long, long, dreary, waiting years shall not any more be heard.

For us who remain the loss is final and fatal; to be endured, but not to be mitigated. But for him how fares it? Ah! for him, even behind death, there is hope. If beyond the grave is no existence, then neither affection availeth any thing nor disaffection. Let us eat and drink, for what signifies aught? But if all our faith be not vain, if not in this life only have we hope in Christ, is it so sure that an evil thing hath happened even to him who was summoned hence in his youth? Doubtless the Creator meant that we should desire life and love many days, that we may see good; yet not to the dead come silence and emptiness, and the grief of a clay-cold body for warmth and breath and beauty. All these he left in leaving life, and passed on to another world to new surroundings, to plans and purposes, to interests and enjoyments as full, as keen, as absorbing as those that engrossed him here; to friendships not more tender, perhaps, but perhaps more wise; to companions and guardians who shall not supplant the old, but who shall satisfy his yearnings and forefend the pangs of loneliness and heart-hunger, and a homesickness of the heavens. Out of life he goes, but into life. The wickedly wanton bullet could smite earth with a lasting sorrow, but it carried no disaster to the skies. The young eye grew dim, and the strong arm failed, and the right hand lost its cunning; but, entering his new world, no power was weakened, no keen possibility was dulled, not a charm was lost, not a grace marred.

"Oh! death, where is thy sting? Oh! grave, where is thy victory?"

But what is it to live a hundred and two years? It is to dwell among the tombs. It is to be the one living out of all the dead; the

one as good as dead among the living. One
after another they disappeared — the friends
of childhood and of youth, parents; then the
past had vanished; brothers, sisters, the friends
of middle years; then self sank out of sight.
Last of all, children died also, and life was
gone. Between the active, glowing world and
this sad survivor is a great gulf fixed, and
who can tell the horror of great darkness that
falls upon him? What wan years stretch before him! What waste places lie around him!
What dim phantoms mock him out of the distant past! What twilight of the mind veils
his future and deadens his aspiration! A
little child playing among the buttercups a
hundred years ago! Was it he? Youth and
maiden—fair-haired, ruddy, shy, and eager—
where are the eyes that shunned his glance?
Whose were the eyes that gazed? What was
it that stirred him so deeply in that long ago?
What fever was in his blood, now so slow and
cold? What made life then so rosy, that is

now so colorless? Oh! vague torment of a
clouded soul! Weary conflict between feeble
memories and the wraiths of the present! In
a vast realm of shadows is there any substance? Through this hell of passivities shines
there any gleam of the heaven of activity?

XI.

WHO IS WHO?

A BRAVE and knightly gentleman of four-score and fourteen years held in his arms a tiny maiden of not one twentieth so many months. He gazed into her blue, steadfast eyes, caressed the silky brown shadow that was fondly called her hair, patted the soft curvature of her cheeks and the dimpled shining shoulders, and said—half musingly and mournfully, looking backward—half tenderly and lovingly, looking forward—"It is Katy; surely it is Katy, plain to see."

Now Katy has been in her grave these eighty years.

Eighty years ago Katy, beloved daughter and sister, in the fresh, full bloom of happy girlhood, paled and faded before the eyes that wept to see, sank away from the hands that

could not hold her, disappeared from a world
that did not miss her, to live only and for ever-
more in hearts whose world was desolated by
her going.

Over that forgotten and unforgotten grave
eighty rolling years have fled. Nearly every
form that trod the earth that day sleeps this
day beneath it. That generation has lapsed
into a silence never to be broken. What they
thought and hoped and planned and loved,
all that they longed for and worked for and
dreaded — to all they are alike indifferent.
Beaming eye and listening ear and throbbing
heart, sturdy strength of sinew, tint of lip and
cheek—the earth has ingulfed them all. They
exist no more but in the sleeping daisy and
the lightly falling snow. But out of the snows
of eighty winters and the daisies of eighty
summers, by what magic art I know not, little
maid Margaret has gathered the eye's light
and the lip's curve, and the chin's dimple and
the cheek's contour of little Great-great-aunt

P

Katy, who gave them into earth's keeping now these fourscore years ago.

Behold, I show you a mystery! But I only show it. I can not explain it. Who can? None, surely, but He who instituted it. What is that wonderful, that incomprehensible law of succession, of inheritance, of transmission, by which qualities, traits, features, go down from father to son, from great-uncle to grand-nephew, from remote ancestor to unseen off-spring? We are so used to it that we are not surprised; but it is, nevertheless, one of the most hidden of secrets. There is some law, but we have not begun to grasp it. That a child should resemble its parents we can al-most persuade ourselves that we understand. Love, we know — nay, even association — but love, surely and strongly, moulds even matur-ity into harmony and even into resemblance. The husband and wife, born and reared far from each other, under circumstances and in a society totally diverse, do sometimes, it is said, come to resemble each other. That abounding mutual attraction which drew them together makes them one in hope and love and purpose and sympathy and heart's desire, and brings presently oneness of expression and feature. This we may fancy that we understand. The children are stamped with the image that each cherishes most fondly. This, too, is not wholly incomprehensible. But, even here, why does one child resemble the father and one the mother, and why is a third totally unlike both ? We only pluck at the skirts of a mystery, and it evades us. And why should this boy have the petulance and passion, the temperament, and even the manners, of a great-uncle whom neither his father nor his mother ever saw, who died in early manhood, and of all the living is remembered now and recalled only by his sister, who sees him reproduced in this little grandson after sixty years of silence and seclusion ? Obedient to what mandate did maid Margaret look through Katy's eyes and smile with Katy's lips so loyally that Floyd went back through all his bitter, busy years, back through his soft Indian summer and his rich harvest-time and the sweet spring sunlight, to his bright boyhood and his young sister's promise? Why do children and children's children go their separate ways to the ends of the earth, marry out and out, grow bronzed by foreign suns and foreign blood, to be in some remote spot recognized as kindred by an alien and a stranger through some peculiar quivering of the eyelid or some singular remembered cadence of the voice? By what law came that eyelid to quiver, that voice to resound through the intermingling and fusion, not to say confusion, of years and zones and families? Why does that one resemblance strain through a thousand differences, and why does it alight only on three or four, and shun the three or four score who have equal claim to its favor?

Are the few resemblances we recognize not

to be compared to the many, unrecognized, which we inherit from forgotten forefathers ? Is it that every trick of feature and trait of character belonged first to some ancestor, only there is no one to tell us who he was ? Are we but eclecticism and conglomeration, a mere second and third hand article — the *disjecta membra* of past generations? Does Nature mock us ? With all our pain and toil and eager endeavor, with all our anguish and anger, ambition and hatred, and hope and love, are we but treading, after all, the old dull round of things ? Has all this mortal agony and unutterable bliss of birth and love and life and death resulted only in this, that what was Katy once is Margaret now—that a man is simply his grandfather ? Then why not let Katy keep on living ? Why not let the grandfather stay grandfather ? Why should Nature be at the pains of so many processes to make three generations, when it would seem that one generation would answer the same purpose with

a great deal less trouble? Why did not
Nature hold out as she began—

> "When Adam lived nine hundred years,
>   Methuselah still more;
> When Enoch very old appears—
>   Seth, Abraham, and Noah?"

And yet these cases may not be at all
to the point. I do not know that the children of these old patriarchs, and their grand-
children and their great-grandchildren, were
any more original than the offspring of their
short-lived descendants. Doubtless as Eve
dandled little Lamech upon her knees she
delighted to see and to point out that in his
forehead he favored Methusael, and that he
had Mehujael's nose, and Irad's eyes, and
the bonnie brown hair of Enoch, and then,
with a deep sigh, she would skip a generation,
and declare that by his sturdy tread and erect
little figure you might know him the wide
world through for Adam's own grandson! We
do not, then, strictly speaking, inherit traits.

We are simply made with like tendencies. Margaret has nothing that Katy ever held, but through some remote, deep-buried law of likeness, out of the dew and blossom of the earth she gathers such a loveliness of outline and color as Katy drew from the young world of hers. Though Katy had lived on till now, Margaret would have been Margaret all the same.

It is to be said in favor of the present order of things, that under it we are alive and ourselves instead of being only our grandfathers or buttercups.

XII.

MOTHERS AS GUARDIANS.

A LOVING missionary mother once said that through all the infancy and childhood of her children she was never free from the dread of that day when she must send them to America to be educated. To the ordinary mind it seems that there is no business in the world so important that parents have a right to give up their children for its sake, whether that business be commerce or fashion or converting the heathen. The heathen are a great way off from us; and in a vast majority of cases are full-grown heathen, and in all cases established heathen nations, before we are so much as aware of their existence. We are not in the least responsible for their being heathen, or for their being at all. But for the little child his parents are responsible. He is their pecul-

iar property, their "charge to keep;" and how
they can justify themselves in giving him in
exchange for any number of aliens and for-
eigners it is difficult to see. What shall it
profit a man if he gain the whole world and
lose his own child? Between a million Mon-
golians—who have been eating with chopsticks
for thousands of years, whom you have to travel half around the world to get at, and who, as
a nation, are likely to go on without any more
perceptible diminution of chopsticks than if
you had stayed at home—and your own child,
whom you have called into existence, and
whose character and fate for this world and
for all worlds lie in your hands, how can there
be any choice? Which has the strongest claim?
I say nothing against pagan claims. I know
that Christ said, Go ye and teach all nations;
but he did not say, Take now thy son and
offer him for a burnt-offering. It is grand
for a man to sacrifice himself; but has he a
right to sacrifice his children? And can any

sacrifice be greater than the loss of their parents? When I think of the shadow that broods over the cradle in so many missionary homes —the shadow of a separation almost worse than death, for it has the sorrows without the immunities of death; a separation which means that you lose out of your home the prattle, the hinderance, the dear waywardness of little children, the brightness of boyhood and girlhood, the ardor of opening life; and that somewhere out of reach the young hearts may be breaking with homesickness, as yours is breaking with childsickness; somewhere the life whose every development is so dear to you, whose very faults only bind you to it closer; somewhere out of sight, out of reach, that life is unfolding to the eye and touch of strangers —thinking of all this, I think of the devotee swinging on his iron hooks. It seems, somehow, a sadder thing to leave one's children from a sense of duty than from recklessness of obligation. It is the torture of hearts made

sensitive by education, conscience, refinement.
I suppose it is noble and unselfish, but I can
not think it right.

Paul, in his charge to Timothy, says: "Thou,
therefore, endure hardness as a good soldier
of Jesus Christ. No man that warreth entan-
gleth himself in the affairs of this life." Of
which the Rev. Albert Barnes, of blessed memory, makes note thus:

"Neither the minister nor the soldier is to
be encumbered with the affairs of this life;
and the one should not be more than the other.
... Roman soldiers were not allowed to marry,
nor to engage in any husbandry or trade....
The general principle was that they were ex-
cluded from those relations, agencies, and en-
gagements which it was thought would divert
their minds from that which was to be the
sole object of pursuit. So with the ministers
of the Gospel. It is equally improper for
them to entangle themselves with the business
of a farm or plantation, with plans of specula-

tion and gain, and with any purpose of worldly
aggrandizement. The minister of the Gospel
accomplishes the design of his appointment
only when he can say with sincerity that he is
not entangled with the affairs of this life."

Mr. Barnes skillfully avoids affirming that
ministers should not marry; but he might as
well have said it outright. He declares that
Roman soldiers were not allowed to marry,
and that it is equally improper for ministers
to entangle themselves. Therefore, ministers
ought not to marry. In this logic can the eye
of faith discern a flaw? Now, with the Œcu-
menical Council fresh in our memories, heaven
forbid that we should go about preaching a
celibate priesthood, or any other peculiar dog-
ma of the Romish Church. But if unadulterated orthodoxy yet exists in the world, it is
surely to be found in Paul's Epistles and
Barnes's Notes; and here they are. It is not
I that speak unto you; but Paul and Mr.
Barnes. Seeing the children of missionaries

torn from their parents; seeing missionaries
bringing their tender little ones from the ends
of the earth, and leaving them to the chance
wisdom and uncertain love of strangers, and
returning over the sea, with heartache and
desolation, I am not so sure but that St. Paul
was right, and that even Mr. Barnes builded
better than he knew.

There are many I know ready to rise and
say that other parents than ministers send their
children abroad to be educated; that missionaries' children are warmly received, tenderly
cared for, very happy, have two homes and
two sets of parents, instead of one, and always
turn out well; that missionaries must give up
country, and it is very hard if they must give
up hearthstone too; and that the family is as
powerful and important a part of the proselyt-
ing influence as the man. Your testimony
may all be true, and your reasoning unim-
peachable; but all the same, as between one's
own children and any number of savages, I

believe the latter ought quick to upfly and kick the beam. And so, spite of pope, priest, and judge, *e pur si muove!*

There are not many, but there are some who respond to this view of the subject with a novel theory. They say:

" The case, as you put it, rests on the most palpable *petitio principii.* You assume that mothers are, *per se,* best qualified to train and rear their own children ; while, in fact, the best thing that could be done for a large portion of the children of the current mothers would be to place them under the care and tutelage of more judicious, not to say more interested persons. Of a large number of the children of missionaries actually known to us who have been reared by their friends in this country, there is not one that has failed of respectability, and some of them have become eminent in worth and usefulness; a result we should not have dared to predict had they been left to the training of their own mothers.

There are thousands of mothers who have fine, bright, healthy children, but who spoil them by neglect or over-indulgence."

" The Supreme Court of the United States may be assumed to know something," said the venerable judge to the young advocate who was cumbering his speech with profuse quotations. There is a common ground on which we all stand, a common starting-point from which we must advance on any line of argument. I admit assuming that mothers are, *per se*, best qualified to train and rear their own children. No proposition seems to be more self-evident. If that is begging the question, mendicancy must be the state of nature; for no question is more ours by honest inference than this. If mothers are not, *per se*, the ones to train and rear their own children, then the whole creation is illogical, instinct is untrustworthy, and there is no call to believe any thing.

Mothers are, indeed, very imperfect. So are

sewing-women and doctors and shoemakers.
But, however injudicious a mother may be in
the management of her child, it is easier to
suppose that it is because she is personally unwise than because she is the wrong person.
Indeed, I think mothers will stand a comparison with members of any profession. The
women of this country make as good mothers
as the men make merchants and ministers, and
no more deserve to have their children taken
from them because they do not bring them up
well than ministers deserve to be turned out
of their pulpits because they do not convert
their people to righteousness and temperance.
When women claim equality with men in mer-
cantile and mechanical accomplishments, we
must return a verdict of " not proven." But
when men charge women with failure in the
one department which they hold by what we
have hitherto supposed divine right, it is only
courtesy which restrains us to so negative a
reply as " not proven." Looking at it from

without, and judging only by results, woman vindicates her right to train her own children just as irrefragably as man vindicates his to traffic and plead and practice.

Looked at from within, the case is equally strong. Nature and revelation alike put the child into the hands of his parents. Indeed, the fact of motherhood seems to be the one divine preparation, sometimes almost the only preparation, for a discharge of its duties. The woman who was frivolous and selfish becomes, with the advent of her little, helpless, tender child, thoughtful, devoted, conscientious. The new life calls out qualities which were never before developed. But doctors of divinity not only reckon motherhood no qualification, but, rather, count it a disqualification. Unless they mean to imply that the women who go out as missionaries are inferior to those who stay at home, that the mothers of our country are inferior to the women who are not mothers, they must mean that the reason why moth-

Q

ers are injudicious is that they are dealing with
their own offspring. That is, the one thing
needful in rearing children is that they should
be some one else's children. "Train up a
child in the way he should go," means always
your neighbor's child. The first thing to do
with your own is, in rustic parlance, "to swap
him off." Let no man seek his own, but every
man another's children.

This is pleasant and piquant. It cuts across
lots with a refreshing directness. Hereafter,
when we see mothers over-indulgent, over-pli-
ant, or in any way injudicious, we shall not
need to devise how the character of woman
shall be improved, her mind enlightened, her
resolution strengthened, her firmness fortified.
It is not that women are weak, vacillating,
short-sighted; that they need to think less of
the present and more of the future; that they
need to be reminded how stern and unyielding
the world will be to their children; and that,
as the mother can not always stand between

her child and the consequences of his evil action, so it is the part of true, wise love to let the child suffer those consequences now, while the evil is small and the penalty light, and his parents stand by to succor and support, rather than shield him now, and leave him to bear by and by alone and unaided the heavy burden of indulgence unlimited and passions uncontrolled. This is a difficult task, hard to be understood or undertaken.   But once establish that there is no inherent propriety in parents rearing their children; that parents have no especial gospel to children, nor children to parents; that the hostelry, rather than the family, is the ideal type of human society; and you have simplified matters amazingly.   It is a great improvement on the divine arrangement.   The Creator seems to have planned it so that parent and child should elevate and educate each other; but what God hath joined together a doctor of divinity does not hesitate to put asunder.   He does it not merely in special cases, which may require special treatment; but he denies that there is any essential bond. In motherhood, *per se*, there is no vital force.

Of course, then, the missionaries are free to give their children over to strangers, while they look after the heathen.

But with a great sum obtained they this freedom.

And if women are not fit to bring up their own children, it remains to be seen what they *are* good for.

"If neglect in this matter," says another, "must be censured, why not point the shaft at those rich and well-to-do mothers who attempt nothing more for their children than to kiss them good-night, and to make sure that they are far enough away in the morning to save themselves from unseasonable disturbance from infantile noise and caresses? If mothers are ever justifiable in finding substitutes in the rearing and training of their children, can a stronger case be presented than

that of the women who must take this course,
or rear their children amid the filth and debasement of heathenism, or leave their poor
husbands without solace or comfort in ungenial climes and under the privations of heathen
communities ?"

It hath been said by them of old time that,
to make hare soup, it is indispensable that
you first catch your hare. Before you point
the shaft at rich and well-to-do mothers, whose
only care is to kiss their children and keep
them out of the way, you must find such
mothers. I never saw any, outside of books.
There is a certain kind of story in which you
encounter fabulous wealth, amid which live
haughty heroines of peerless beauty, who suddenly change their wedding-days for the purpose of showing their power over their lovers,
and who come very near losing them in consequence, but who are generally saved by the
skin of their teeth.   In such narratives you
do sometimes meet the unnatural mother who

spends her life in a vain show, while the se-
raphic Seraphina, her lovely young daughter,
is given over to the ignorant but fond and
faithful Bridget, by whom she is, strangely
enough, nurtured into entrancing womanhood.
But I hereby depose and say that I never met
any of these persons. I never saw any mother, however rich and well-to-do, who was open
to the charge of neglect or indifference re-
garding her children. On this point there is
no distinction between rich and poor. Mothers, as a class—and, to my observation, without exception—are, in point of affection, care,
fidelity, perfect. I do not say that they are
always judicious, always sagacious. Very far
from it. But what they fail in is wisdom, not
love. They are injudicious because they do
not know what is the best thing to do, or lack
nerve to do it; not because they are too selfish or self-indulgent to do it. Any man who,
in a world of wickedness and weakness, points
his shafts at mothers for neglect of this sort

is simply wasting his ammunition, and deserves, so far, to be classed among Dotty Dimple's "nidiots." The poorest mother in this
land is not more devoted to her children than
the richest. The lowest mother is not more
careful than the highest. Through every grade
of society — throughout the aristocracy of
wealth, literature, and politics, just as truly
and thoroughly as in the ranks of mediocrity
and poverty—the first thought of mothers is
for their children. The greatest benefit of
wealth or rank in this country is reaped by
the young, in the increased opportunity furnished for education and accomplishments.

Even that *bête noir*, the woman's rights
woman, is thoroughly innocent of the accusa-
tion of neglect of family. Not a particle of
proof has ever been introduced to show that
the children of the platform are not as well
cared for as those of any other department of
society, while a great many facts have inci-
dentally disproved it. Even the missionary

women, who send their children away from themselves, do it not from dislike, but from a sense of duty, which, at the very worst that can be said, is but a mistake.

Love for her children is rooted and grounded in the mother, and brings forth fruit of care and watch and patience and toil, from which no lot is exempt. I should feel myself a slanderer in the first degree were I to breathe a single aspersion against the sentiment, the intent, the endeavor of mothers.

As for the women who must employ substitutes, or rear their children amid the filth and debasement of heathenism, the very point in question is whether they have any right to create the necessity for substitutes. Have they a right deliberately to surround their children with this filth and debasement? Nor is there any comparison between the rich mother and the missionary mother. The rich mother does not find substitutes. She finds assistants, as she needs must and ought, to the ad-

vantage of all classes; but I have yet to see
the mother who abused her wealth by giving
her child in exchange. Wealth and position
impose their own duties—duties which often
interfere with the companionship, solace, and
entertainment to be had from children; and
these duties are just as sacred and just as im-
perative as any imposed upon the missionary.
Do we owe less to our own country than we
owe to Micronesia? Are we any more bound
to elevate Ah Sing than John Smith? The
woman who goes to Zanguebar with her husband, and spends her life as a useful missionary, is worthy of great respect, even if she
does send relays of children to America, to be
taken care of and supported by other people. But the woman who stays in New York,
and brings up her own children, and does all
she can to be agreeable and intelligent in
New York circles, is worthy of equal respect.
And because she dresses well, and cultivates
art, and entertains strangers, and dines at sev-
en, she does not forfeit our respect. As for

sacrifices, and ungenial climes, and heathen
privations, let us not so much as hear of them.
The world is one, and women go to China and
Japan because, on the whole, they choose to
go.   I question if the mass of missionary
women make more daily personal sacrifice, or
have a harder and more exacting, while they
certainly have a more stimulating life, than
the mass of women who stay at home.   I question if the female missionaries of China or
Armenia work more unremittingly, or have
greater obstacles to encounter in their domestic affairs, or greater privation of comfort, than
the farmers' wives of New England.   And
as for ungenial climates, one would say that
from the pleasant summer haunts and heights
of Asia our missionary brethren could afford
to smile down upon us a smile that is child-
like and bland when we talk of ungenial cli-
mate, with our water-pipes freezing and bursting on Thanksgiving-day, and Cochituate Lake
threatening to be stone-dry under no especial
provocation !

XIII.

HOME WAYS AND FOREIGN WAYS.

SATAN, who finds some mischief still for idle hands to do, takes exception to the fact that city mothers send their children to the parks in charge of nurses, instead of following the example of those foreign mothers who sojourn among us, and themselves accompany their children. Mothers are warned of the carelessness, neglect, and cruelty of these hired nurses, and of the danger to which the little ones are exposed in person, in association, and in habits.

That the character of those persons to whom little children are intrusted is of the gravest importance no one will deny. But to say or to imply that mothers are not to feel that they have done the whole duty of woman unless they stand by the baby carriage or watch the

little romps themselves is to advance a theory
so impracticable as to destroy our respect for
the judgment and our interest in the opinions
of those who originated it. No doubt the hap-
piest life of all is that which gives to the mother constant supervision without misgiving or
undue self-sacrifice. I know a baby who took
his nap every day in the corn-field. On pleasant mornings he was enshrined on his basket-
throne among the pillows and set adrift. Whoever came by took a turn at the baby carriage.
Now he was rattling along the gravel walk,
now he was cooing in the grove; but always,
moving or at rest, in the fresh open air. When
sleep came he was rolled into the corn-field,
where the tall stalks sheltered him from the
sun, and rustled him the sweetest lullabies.
Father and mother and field-hands and children and chickens and big dog shared with the
nurse a living watch over him till he awoke to
new joys with the very spring of life in his
veins.

But it is not given to every baby, alas! to be born in groves and corn-fields. The cities are full of boys and girls playing in the streets thereof. Perhaps the best thing a city can do for its children is to lay out great parks for them to play in. There the rich and the poor may meet together, and for the one and for the other alike is the turf green, and the waters sparkle, and the broad trees cast their friendly shade. There the children can not come too often or stay too long. But if the conscientious, devoted, and all-too-anxious American mother is to feel that she must not permit her children to go unless she can attend them, or to remain in the parks without her, their freedom of range must be pitifully curtailed. She is careful and troubled about many things. Society and sewing and a thousand household duties crave her attention and claim her time. I wish, indeed, this were not so. I wish she were lighter of heart and of foot, more free from care, more easily persuaded to leisure and

open-air enjoyment. But the pleasure she will
not permit herself she will secure for her child's
health. And this is right. For Heaven's sake
let us not now set a stumbling-block even in
this path! To say that children must not play
in the parks without their mothers is simply
saying that they shall not play there at all. No
woman who is what she ought to be in her
family and in society can afford to spend in
the park as much time as her children ought
to spend there. It would be a waste to herself and to the world, and not least to her children. The true way is that which most mothers adopt, of sending the children out with a
trustworthy nurse. A merchant might just as
wisely undertake to keep his accounts himself
as a woman to be every moment in attendance
on her children. It is not economy, but extravagance of the most wanton sort. The utmost care should be exercised in selecting a
nurse; and no day passes in which a mother
should not be watchful of her children, her

nurse, and all their ways. We hear occasionally of instances of cruelty, neglect, and injury
which show this; but we hear far oftener of
forgeries, defalcations, and breaches of trust
which show the danger incurred by bankers in
employing clerks and cashiers. Nobody, however, draws the moral that clerks and cashiers are to be dispensed with, and bankers are
to do the book-keeping themselves. We say
only that they and the directors and the president should perform more thoroughly their
own duty of inspection and supervision. The
ordinary nurse is under no stronger tempta-
tion to neglect than the ordinary cashier is to
cheat. Perhaps it is not offensive to say that a
woman is more inclined to be tender and loving to a child than a man is to be just to a
man, so that it is no harder for a woman to
find a faithful woman than it is for a man to
find a faithful man. Let the mothers, then,
continue to send their children a-field with tried
and trusty nurses, assured that in ninety-nine

cases out of a hundred their own vigilance is ample to insure a vigilant care of the little ones, and that the danger incurred by the children is out of all ratio with the danger they would incur by being left within-doors till such time as the mothers can take them out.

When it comes to contrasting American with foreign mothers, I am more than skeptical. There is not on earth a more devoted and self-sacrificing being than the American mother. A foreigner is held up to our country-women for an example because she accompanies her child into the park. I have seen her on her winding way. The carriage stops at the park gates, madame alights, the nurse alights, the footman alights, the secretary—to whom the child has taken a fancy—alights, and they saunter up and down the graveled walks in assiduous attendance upon the little two-year-old. I fancy our country would be pleased to see the clerks of its public offices detailed to nurse the children of the public officers. But

apart from that, is this child, surrounded by def-
erent adults, really better off than the crowd
of children on the greensward turning somer-
saults, jumping rope, trundling hoop, rolling
and running and leaping and tumbling in the
wild freedom and frolic of childhood, with
two or three nurses gossiping on the benches,
and seeing that the young republic receive no
detriment?

It is not necessary to believe that we are
the people, and that wisdom will die with us.
Neither is it necessary to assume that the mon-
archies of Europe are actually effete, and that
her institutions have bred only decay in all
the departments of human life. America and
Europe, let us sagely admit, have each its pe-
culiarities, which are in their way admirable.
Doubtless, too, Asia and Africa are not wholly wrong and irrational in many customs which
we should be slow to adopt. But while it is
unreasonable and childish to decry manners
simply because they are foreign, it is certainly

not reasonable and manly to adopt them for
the same reason. As between the two it seems
rather more respectable to grumble against every thing un-English, as the English are said
to do, than it is to be ready to drop your own
ways and run after those of other countries, on
the assumption that they are more refined and
desirable, and that to live after the manner of
Europeans, and not of Americans, is to be cosmopolitan and cultured.

For instance, in Europe social life is more
circumscribed in certain respects than in America. On the Continent children and young
girls, and even young ladies, are not accustomed to go into the street without a nurse or
other attendant. In England there is less re-
striction ; yet even there the Maggie Greys
are brought to account for having driven alone
with the Mr. Traffords to the Bois de Bou-
logne, and only wonder what would be said if
it were known that they received calls from
these gentlemen when the Mrs. Berrys are out.

No one disputes the propriety of these customs in the countries where they originate. It is doubtless not without reason that girls are protected abroad. That reason unhappily is that men are so bad that such protection is needed against them. It is matter of evidence that American girls, thoughtlessly and innocently following in Paris American customs, are misunderstood and insulted. That is a reason why they should do in Rome as the Romans do, but not why they should bring Roman ways to Boston. It is the glory of America that her men hold her women in honor. As a fact of the most commonplace character, young girls can walk down Beacon Street and Broadway and Pennsylvania Avenue from morning till night not only without insult, but without attracting any special attention. Little girls can play in the parks without nurses and without danger, except such danger as comes any where from crowded streets or reckless drivers; that is, if I may say so, without moral danger.

Why, then, should we assume a weakness and wickedness which we do not possess? Since our way of life has given us a society in which young ladies do drive with young gentlemen, and do receive calls from young gentlemen, without in the least degree detracting from either their dignity or their delicacy, why should we not continue to build ourselves with strength in that direction rather than put up barriers of weakness after the Continental fashion? I think the best men and the best women of this country are not only as strong, but as fine and noble, as the best Europeans. I think the rank and file compare very favorably with the rank and file of any country. It is therefore extremely painful to see our people of culture and travel doing any thing that looks toward distrusting or deteriorating the inward self-respect and self-control, and quiet, unspoken, but universal faith in those qualities, which is, perhaps, the distinguishing feature of our society, and substituting for it out-

ward guards. I like to see little children playing by themselves wherever it is safe, and not
simply where it is fashionable to play by themselves. When I see a tall boy led around by
a nurse, I do not feel " Here is a young gentleman carefully educated," but "Here is a molly-
coddle." The native American young gentleman is doubtless at this moment " shinning" up
an apple-tree, or sliding and striding down the
rough stone balustrade of the front door-step
to the great detriment of the knee-breeches
which he has not yet outgrown ; but he is not
more likely to grow up into a *petit maître* than
the much-benursed young gentleman, and the
chances are also that he will have some occupation beyond boxing, billiards, and riding to
hounds. When a young girl is guarded against
dangers which do not exist, the chances are
not that she will be more delicate and exquisite thereby, but that she will be more affected
and unreal. If we adopt foreign customs in
preference to our own, let us do it because they

are convenient, effective, or otherwise desirable, not because they are foreign.

When Ralph the Heir is putting force upon
himself to marry Polly Neefit, his breeches-
maker's daughter, he wonders within himself
whether, after they are married, he shall ever
be able to make her call her father " papa."
Now in England the true Shibboleth of high
breeding may be whether you give your mother her proper natural-history classification as a
mammalian, or whether you call her by the
ancient name of mother; but in this country
it is not so. In many families, and some communities of good birth and breeding, *papa* and
mamma are common terms. Others of equal
claims to refinement know only fathers and
mothers. I confess to a liking for the more
universal, and perhaps homely, but certainly poetical, Saxon. It is nervous and strong.
Papa and *mamma* suit well the infant lips that
frame to pronounce them so quickly, and from
which they come as fresh and clear as bab-

bling brooks; but they always seem like babble. Grown men and women referring to their papas and mammas remind one of bibs and ankle-tie shoes. Yet doubtless this is mere matter of habit, and people who have grown up with their papas and mammas find them as dignified as any father and mother. But what is puerile and ridiculous is for the " paw " and " maw " of a merry and sensible Southern or Middle State family, or the father and mother of a sober down-East household, to find themselves, after a year or so of cosmopolitan society or Continental travel, suddenly transmuted into papa and mamma. And when this papafied and mammalized family returns to its native community—a community in which every individual approaching adult age does very nearly every thing which is right in his own eyes, and attains an average rectitude quite equal to that of the family which is cribbed, cabined, and confined by strict European laws —when the grown-up daughters of this family of American citizenship and foreign travel suddenly discover the necessity of asking " mamma's permission " every time they wish to go down town to buy a yard of ribbon or a sheet of music, the situation is not without humor in the eyes of the quaint untraveled Yankee.

The same class of critics admire the superior simplicity of the dress of our foreign children over our silken-clad home products. They lament the mysterious disappearance of little girls from our civilization. We have small women, it is said, bedizened like their mothers in silks and flounces, dressed up, or down, into an insipid and constrained prematurity. But the little girl — free, bright, child-like, natural — is gone.

Oh no ! We deceive ourselves. We overrate our own power, and underrate the strength of nature. There is extravagance, I grant. Lack of independence, taste, character, does sometimes put little girls into unbecoming finery, but not so often as we think.

I have been in the very French schools whose
extravagant American dressing is deplored and
contrasted with the substantial plainness of the
foreign pupils in them, and I have seen not a
single silk gown on the benches.   I meet the
little lasses on their way to and fro, and very
pretty they look, with their fresh frocks and
white aprons, and sailor hats jauntily posed
above their "bhanged" hair, and swinging
satchels sawing the air—but one silk gown
have I not seen.

"Opal," I say to a *pensionnaire*, "do the
girls wear silk dresses at your school?"

"No," says she, carelessly; and adds, "only
Emma Paine has an old one made over."

Pray believe me, Sir Critic, your eyes deceive you.   The American mothers dress their
little ladies so daintily and tastefully that you
are won away from your judgment, and mistake taste and skill for cost—the flash of cambric for the sheen of silk.   If I were a betting
man, I would not be afraid to wager my whole

fortune that every silk worn on ordinary school occasions by an American girl is an old gala dress of her own or her mother's, remade by Buttrick's patterns and the sewing-machine, too much worn for state occasions, but still too strong to be wholly thrown aside; and that its appearance on the school-bench is therefore a measure of economy, and not of extravagance.

We do weak and wrong and foolish things enough. So much the more let not our good be evil-spoken of.

And the little girl too, God bless her! is made of sterner stuff than to be so easily extinguished. It would take more silk and satin than our ships can bring to stiffen her into a reliable and proper monotony. She is often subdued, but she is constantly breaking out in insurrection. She views her clothes with a suitable reverence, but there are moments, and even hours, of supreme indifference. Only this morning she came into the post-office while I was there. She had doffed her trump-

ery over-skirts, for even the American little
girl is not without a plain undress suit.   She
wore a big blue coat and cape, over which her
yellow hair tossed in waves and waterfalls of
sunshine.   In her tiny fist she clinched a letter which she was to deposit.   By utmost
stretch of tiptoe she could hardly bring her
bit of a nose to a level with the counter, behind which stood the young clerk; but full of
her important mission, too young to be bashful,
regardless of the men who lingered over their
papers and their chit-chat around the stove,
and intent only on her errand, she managed
to transfer her letter to the clerk's outstretched hand; then bustling out of the door, which
she could with difficulty open, she cried, with
her clear, shrill, child voice, "Now, Benny, you
make that letter *go*, 'cause I want it to *go!*"
Evidently she considered the whole postal service of the United States dependent on Benny's
good-will.   But here was a real little girl—
just as real as if she had been born a century

ago—real in her intentness, her simplicity, her imperiousness, her fearlessness — real in the eager smile that saw no one, and thought of nothing but to rush home and prove that she had done her errand—just as real as when she sits on the floor singing and rocking her doll to sleep, and "does wish Susie wasn't so *un- fond* of 'Shoo, Fly.'"

And just a little way beyond me in the western winter sunshine there is another little girl. She has all the furbelows there is any call for, but the little girl is unmarred, the little soul is uncrimped, unstarched, free of fashion or formula. Bless your heart! if you could have seen how bravely she fought her lady mother in the broad aisle the other day! It would have done your very soul good—you who fancy the little girl has been over-dressed into propriety. Lady mother evidently had doubts of Patty's behavior in Sunday-school, and wanted her to go where she could be steadily supervised; but Patty, too, had rights

which she knew, and knowing, dared maintain, and insisted, *pugnis et calcibus*, on going
into the little girls' class, and did go, and sat
upright with a demure propriety which must
have planted a sting in the maternal conscience. All her feathers and fooleries had
not quenched the irrepressible sturdiness which
glows in the bosom of the little girl, and she
stood her ground with as much spirit and per-
sistence as if she had been clad in a tow slip.

Daisy comes softly stealing into the parlor
where her mother sits with guests, and pucker-
ing her rosy lips into her mother's ear, asks in
loud, outraged whispers, "Mamma, *thall* I wear
my blue thath? It dothn't correthpond!" The
unregenerate male mind, overhearing the in-
quiry, is amazed, not to say awed. A five-
year-old maiden already versed in the science
of correspondences is a precocity not dreamed
of in Swedenborg's philosophy. But be not
alarmed. Daisy's immortal nature is not wholly given up to "thathes," nor does it appear

to be materially deteriorated by the consciousness that all colors are not harmonious in combination.   This knowledge is often a matter
of instinct, and though Daisy is a connoisseur
in fitnesses, she has a soul above "thathes;"
and, for all her dainty dressing, she can upon
occasion forget her decorum, and rage into as
pretty a passion as the most conservative could
desire.

Harry is not a girl.   That is, he will cease
to be in a year or two; but now, in white
frock and petticoats, he is girl enough to look
at.   The same ruffling and embroidery that
spoil his sisters wreak their full wrath on him.
Is he spoiled?   His picture lies before me,
just taken.   Apparently he trotted into the
photographer's on his own account.   He is
capable of such things.   No mother's hand arranged him for immortality.   His little legs
hang bowed in stolid repose.   The last tree or
shrub has done harm to his cambric flounce.
His dimpled hands lie in a blur of satisfaction

and unconsciousness; and his fat wrists are not in the least abashed by obtruding half-way out of what must have been originally long sleeves, but which the arms seem ere-while to have outgrown. That sash—*Ilium fuit!*—I knew it in its pristine brilliancy, but it has been as familiar with soap-suds as the white frock, and is a standing proof that silk will wash. But what cares Harry, and what care I? The sturdy, strong little body is there, the brave, bright, handsome face, wearing yet only its inherited features, " the crown where-with his mother crowned him," and we know not what shall be. But he is not spoiled. That plump, solemn face, fixed now with un-wonted steadfastness, will brighten over a new frock. I have seen the great eyes snap, and heard the young voice shriek with delight, at a gay suit; but it was a surface joy. The child underneath goes his way strong in in-fantile vigor.

No, the children are still here. The little

girls have not left us. Do not let us tremble at bugbears. We may stifle them all we can under superfluous and incongruous decorations; we may dress them like dolls, and bemoan ourselves that they have turned into dolls, but all around the little elfs are laughing us to scorn. Beneath all their flimsy fussery the wild, willful, fantastic creatures are playing their fantastic tricks, laughing and crying, fibbing and fretting, romping and teasing, weaving their wonderful imaginings, fighting their infantile battles, doing their best to resist our encroachments, neutralize our folly, defy our ignorance, and to grow up into frank, natural, delightful men and women. It is a losing game, the more's the pity. By continued trituration we shall worry them all down to pretty much one model of commonplace, and by the time they are grown up we shall wonder what could have made their childhood so winsome; but during their short spring-time the little girls are out in full blossom.

I think the reason of our sad wandering is that we are not careful to see accurately. We mistake inference upon slight induction for sufficient and actual observation. We glance and report. We do not watch.

A reviewer, speaking of the late Sir Henry Holland, remarked that " in his published ' Recollections' he tells his readers that he never knew a great misfortune, that he never felt much sorrow—the death of his wife, in 1866, being the severest trial he ever experienced." But those who thought it worth while to remember so trifling a matter as the death of a wife, remembered too that this wife was the eldest daughter of the Rev. Sydney Smith. Her going did not give her husband much sorrow, but her coming gave her father great pleasure. She herself has told us that as the time approached for the birth of this, his first child, he constantly expressed his wish, first, that it might be a daughter, and, secondly, that she might be born with one eye, that he might

S

never lose her. She came with two eyes, but was just as warmly welcomed as if she had not possessed the undesired redundancy. In fact, the delighted young father stole her away speedily, to the nurse's horror, and displayed her in triumph to Lord Jeffrey and the future Edinburgh Reviewers.

Then came, says the same dearly loved daughter, such meditations, consultations, and discussions as would not be believed on the all-important matter of her name. Finally, not being able to find one to his taste, her father determined to invent one; and out of all researches and devices came at last the simple and not especially euphonious, yet sufficiently strong and characteristic, name of *Saba*.

So little Saba flourished and grew fat till she was six months old, when the croup seized her with such fearful violence that it defied all the remedies employed by the best medical man that could be obtained. The danger increased with every hour, she tells us. Dr.

Hamilton, then one of the most eminent medical men in Edinburgh, was sent for, could not come, but ordered them to "persevere in giving two grains of calomel every hour; I never knew it fail." It was given for eleven hours. She grew constantly worse. The medical man, as Lady Holland calls him, when we should say *doctor* — her term sounds too much like John Chinaman's "Melican man" — the medical man in attendance then said, "I dare give no more; I can do no more. The child must die; but at this age I would not venture to give more to my own child." But the fond father would not give up. He said to the timid physician, "You can do no more. Hamilton says, Persevere. I will take the responsibility; I will give it to her myself." He gave it, and the child was saved.

I thought if the little longed-for daughter who had been paraded with such foolish, fond, sweet exultation at a very early stage of her existence had struggled out of the world after six months of sunny life, her nearest friend among the survivors would not have said that he never knew a great misfortune, that he never felt much sorrow. I thought the little six-months maiden would have left a sorrow deep and lasting.

She did not die, but lived—lived in an atmosphere of tender love and admiration and cherishing. When she was a woman grown a suitor came in the person of Dr. Holland. The pleased father seems to have quite forgotten his jesting wish that he might never lose his daughter, in satisfaction with the excellent match she was about to make. "We are about to be married," he writes to Lady Holland, "and Saba will be one day Lady Holland. She must then fit herself up with Luttrells, Rogerses, and John Russells, etc.; Sydney Smith she has." In the summer he welcomed Dr. Holland's three children as if they had been his own to spend the whole autumn in his house.

So she who had been a most loving, beloved, and dutiful daughter in her father's house, and who can hardly be supposed to have turned about, and become a selfish and unlovely wife, lived with Dr. Holland thirty-two years, and died; and her husband, who possessed so many charms of manner and disposition, tells us that he never in his life knew a great misfortune or felt much sorrow.

But he lost a wife twice. He had three young children when he married Saba Smith. One would say that the death of a young wife and mother, leaving three forlorn little ones, might make a slight impression on her husband, might seem even to be worthy the name of a great misfortune, might produce something that could be called much sorrow. If she were a bad and worthless woman, her life and her motherhood were a great misfortune. If she were good, what could her death and their orphanage be?

Is it worth while with pains and care to polish a jewel that is to be so thoughtlessly worn, so lightly lost?

So far I had written, dipping my pen in gall not half bitter enough, when the thought came to me: It is impossible. Sir Henry Holland never said any such thing. Sydney Smith was a man demonstratively fond of his family, and it stands to reason that his daughter's husband must have been a human being with a certain sense of propriety and of dignity. Moreover, Sir Henry was a gentleman and a man of society, and of too much acuteness to make so stolid and clumsy a statement as this, apart from any lack of sensibility. To the law and to the testimony. Out of his own mouth shall this beloved physician be condemned, or he shall not be condemned at all. I sent for the "Recollections," the book from which his critic drew the offensive remark, and found that from these "Recollections" Sir Henry formally excludes all family history! He scarcely mentions either death or marriage. The ab-

surdity, the ridiculousness, the *naïveté* of his
statement rest wholly with the newspaper re-
porter who made it. He himself says nothing
of the kind. He makes but two allusions to
his wife in the whole book, and these, though
very tender, are but remote allusions. He
does not say that the death of his wife was
the severest trial he ever experienced. He
does not say that his wife died, or that he
ever had any wife. What he says, with simplicity, dignity, and sufficiency, is this: "I
have much cause to say, on thus looking back
upon it, that my life has been a prosperous
and happy one. *But for the loss—inevitable
as time goes on—of many endeared to me by
the ties of family and friendship, I might
fairly speak of it as untouched up to this
moment by any serious misfortune.*"

Once two gentlemen of eminent abilities,
spotless character, and all lovable qualities,
were discussing theology in the parlor. Forth
from the hands of her tiring-maid came a

damsel of two years, fair as the morning, all
sash and cambric and curls, all ravishing with
daintiness and purity and sweetness of soul
and body. I am no indiscriminate advocate
of child-worship. Children are often ugly,
unattractive, disagreeable, and to be kept out
of sight and sound; but this little atom floated
into the great hall like a sunbeam, and I led
her into the parlor and stood back to watch
the surprise. She trotted about on her two
little musical feet, and her silky curls fluttered, and her blue eyes danced, and her little
figure shone all over with heaven's own light—
and to her and of her those two men spoke
never a word. Then, filled with rage and
despair, I drew her under the very eyes of
the mighty theologian, and he looked upon
her, and said, "Oh! ah!—Still, if moral ability combines with original sin in respect of
justification, adoption, and sanctification—"
went directly on with the argument, just the
same as if an angel had not descended from

the skies to give them light; and I said within
my heart, "It is of no use. The good God
made them, and I suppose he made them
as perfect as would answer, and we must put
up with it — after having used all possible
means to discipline them to better things."
Apparently they are but rudimentary beings.

"Her 'prentice hand she tried on man."

The very best and most gifted among them
have but an imperfect development. A man-
child left to himself bringeth his mother and
sister and wife and all his female well-wishers
to shame, and a man left to himself never
ceases to be more or less a child.

This fable teaches why it is not good for
man to be alone; why he, so much more than
woman, needs a help meet for him, that his
eyes may be opened, that he may discern between the good and the evil.

XIV.

BABY-TALK.

WHEN the new town-house was taken, the nursery was appointed for the top of the house. It was sightly and airy and spacious, full of light and sunshine. From it the noble domes and slender spires, even the far hills and the winding river, were clearly visible; and high up above library and drawing-room and dining-room the children could make as much noise as they pleased, arrange their playthings in all that disorder which is dear to the infantine heart, and pursue the momentous affairs of life without running the risk of interference from trivial, frivolous, and capricious elders. Truly it was a happy thought, this establishing the nursery at the top of the house.

But only a happy thought. For practical

results it would seem that the nursery is the one place the children will not go to. A line of stereoscopic views reaches down every staircase. All the chairs in the chambers are marshaled into one railroad train, and I am allowed a cricket to sit on only by sufferance. My own room is invaded, my best shawl converted into a tent, all my pretty little Shakespeares serve as building-blocks, and I am only too happy if I am not myself pressed into service as architect. There are children under the dining-room table, children behind the sofa, children in the china-closet, and, as I live, there is Baby-in-Breeches at this moment dragging The Other Baby out of the best drawing-room cabinet, where they have been snugly bestowed at hide-and-seek! House-top nursery indeed! You may turn it into a servants' room, or a billiard-room, or a studio, but the children are bubbling all over the house, and never by any accident deviate into the house-top, unless, possibly, a bust in clay is waiting there its transition to marble, in which case undoubtedly Baby-in-Breeches will catch the general spirit of criticism, and " think that eyebrow too high, papa," and stick a billiard cue into it by way of definition, at the cost of an hour's reconstruction by the patient artist.

It is a disorderly and reprehensible custom, this overflow of the children beyond all bounds, this determined onset of sturdy irrepressibles; but it can not be denied that thus we do get delightful and unexpected flashes of fresh individual nature.

I go into the blue room of an errand, and behold! Star-Eyes curled up on the middle of the bed, asleep, under a damask napkin. Presently in my neighboring room I hear a velvet voice calling " Cusnabe!" I hold my peace, to see whereunto this thing will grow. Twenty times she calls " Cusnabe!" in every variety of soft intonation, evidently experimenting on her own voice. Then a thud, a pause, patter, patter, patter, and in she shines, all dewy with sleep, only a little snip of cambric falling off her shoulders, but her fine clothes tucked under her arm and dropping along the way. Then, without a word, without invitation from me, without the least sign of encouragement, she climbs into my lap as calmly as if she owned me, and unto this end was I born, and for this cause came I into the world; and the very assurance and assumption, which in a grown person would be intolerable, in her are simply adorable. Are shyness and shame, then, merely conventionalities? Who shall teach Star-Eyes the dividing line between the charm of self-assertion and the charm of self-withdrawal? No one, indeed; for in the swift-coming years swiftly will come to her the tremors of self-distrust and timidity and dread of encroachment; but as yet her universal confidence, her absolute impossibility of intrusion, are her guarantee of winsomeness.

And now her mantle of sleep falls off from

her, and the blue eyes wander about the room.
They meet a paper doll on the bureau.
"Whose is that *naice* 'ittle doll?"

"It is yours. It was sent to you in a letter."

Then ho! for the bureau, and ho! for
all the rest of the house; and gathering up
her bestrewn garments in a straggling bunch
under her arm, down the stairs she creeps
cautiously, and is soon again deep in the
mysteries of life.

Baby-in-Breeches is fond of his sister after
a high and mighty fashion. When he is gloved
and booted and close-buttoned to the chin in
all the dignity of going out to spend the day,
he turns back after the door is closed to hug
her and kiss her and ejaculate "Pretty creature!" Yet she comes in from her play in the
yard quite pale and agitated, and presses up
against me close, as she asks, eagerly, "*Will*
Prince Butler snap Starry's legs off?" Prince
Butler is the warlike dog of a warlike general

around the corner. And that little rogue of a
Baby-in-Breeches has been telling her that
Prince Butler will snap her legs off! Telling
her? He tells her under my very eyes. He
leaves his sweetest tidbit at the table to come
round and whisper his awful screed to Star-
Eyes. But Star-Eyes has found a way to turn
his flank, and now, when the miscreant approaches her with his Gorgons and chimeras
dire, she simply puts up her own face—"*Will*
Prince Butler snap Starry's legs off?"

"No, indeed."

Whereupon, turning to her Evil-Suggester,
she annihilates him with her "*No, indeedy.*"

And the little wretch even dares to practice
upon me. "Cusnabe," he says, as he stands
contemplating his various expressions in the
great looking-glass, "I climbed a tree in the
Park to-day."

"Oh no! you *did* not dare to climb a tree
and break your legs?"

"Yes, I did. Dangerous tree, too!"

Who wonders that man's inhumanity to man makes countless thousands mourn, when Five-year-old instinctively enhances his pleasures by the mental torture of his inferiors? I do not think we give men half credit enough for their goodness — for their magnanimity and tenderness and benevolence—when they have these qualities. We do not know what up-hill work their attainment is to the natural male mind. We little think what longings to be cruel he has overcome who has learned to be merciful, what spasms of self-denial have gone to the upbuilding of grace in him who was the man-child of nature.

It is a momentous occasion when Star-Eyes is first admitted to the family table during the temporary absence of Nurse. Her docility is pathetic. "Star-Eyes must not put her hands on the table," and off they go. "Fold your hands, Star-Eyes," and the fat little darling hands are folded with a solemnity of expression fully adequate to a doctorate of divinity.

I do not wish to use the word humbug, but
this poor midget is tricked by nature into be-
lieving that her deportment at table is an important matter. I wonder if the same rule
holds good with us. Are there higher classes
of beings to whom our peccadilloes seem as
phenomenal, as innocent, as interesting, as hers
seem to us? She folds her hands demurely,
and is wondrous attractive in the attitude;
but Baby-in-Breeches is eagerly thrusting both
fists into the strawberries and cream, to the
imminent peril of table-cloth and jacket, and
the annihilation of propriety; and though in
the interest of good morals he must be re-
proved, his eager unconventionalism, his absolute unconsciousness, are not less attractive.
And what is his unquestioning obedience of
Star-Eyes but natural virtue? Her sphere
is limited. Society and morality, speaking
through their authorized representative, impose upon her the law of sitting with folded
hands, and that law she unhesitatingly obeys,

and will obey till she is demoralized by bad
example.   That is, when she finds all the rest
of us reaching forth our thumbs to pick out
the plums, she will unfold her own thumbs,
and explore and exploit; but at present she
has no designs in her inmost heart but a complete and devout observance of law.   There
may be such a thing as original sin, but the
sin that I see most of is acquired sin.

It is Sunday, and what shall the Babies do?
Railroad trains of chairs, and Prince Butler,
the dog, can not be allowed on Sunday, that is
certain.   Star Eyes can be left to herself, for
of herself is she never boisterous, but Little-
Breeches esteemeth not one day above another.
He is fond of pictures, however, and will listen
to reading with an almost startling intentness,
gazing into the face of the reader with a wide-
eyed eagerness, as if he

> " Drew
> With one long look your whole soul through
> Your lips, as sunlight drinketh dew."

A picture of "Joseph Sold by his Brethren" serves as text for a long sermon on—well, it must be confessed, on camels as much as on Joseph. Then I say, " Now, if you will get me a Bible, I will read you the story of Joseph."

" The Bible is lost," says he solemnly.

" Oh, no. I think you can find a Bible in the book-case."

" Yes," he says, with renewed and increasing emphasis, " there has been a Bible lost out of this house. It says:

> " 'Saw young Anna Faber
> Come walking into church.' "

Blessed and beloved apostle! Sweetest saint in all the calendar! Worthy successor of that disciple whom Jesus loved, gentlest and tenderest of all the Sons of Thunder, *I* should not have dared to follow my heart's promptings and class you with those holy men of old; but when out of the mouth of babes and sucklings your praise is perfected, it is not for me to stand by and say them nay.

So Little - Breeches is presently convinced that it is a volume of Whittier, and not the Bible, that is lost out of this house, and he starts off on a tour of exploration. Bibles are not so scarce that he need take a Sabbath-day's journey, but his views are vague, his mind is discursive, and his search prolonged.

Presently, after long silence, a hollow voice resounds from some remote fastness—" Cusnabe! *I* don't care to hear 'bout Moses!" And the culprit heaves in sight with a big kaleidoscope, which was put on an upper shelf in a dark closet for the express purpose of keeping it out of his way. So that is the reason why "Moses" was so soon nipped in the bud; but what possessed him to go Bible-hunting in a clothes-closet?

And what feeling is it, what divine discontent with the established order of things, that makes him come in and throw himself in a chair, with his back to the front, and his heels as high up the back as the supply will permit?

Is it a physical or a mental, a nervous or a
social solace, that this attitude ministers to his
perturbed spirit?

And what becomes of his clothes? Oh!
his jackets! Oh! his knees! Oh! the seat
of his trousers! "Little-Breeches has gone out
without his jacket, and will certainly get his
death o' cold!" says Ann, coming in and holding up the mite of a jacket she has found.
"No, Ann, do you not see that is his best jacket, and he has on his old one?"

His best! But what a scarred old veteran it
looks! And if this is the jacket, how then
shall the trousers appear—those eight pairs of
absurd little knee-breeches which it was fondly
hoped would bear him triumphantly through
the summer months and through the Indian
summer till the nipping frosts appeared.
Alas! before the Ides of August the daylight
shone through them.

As for his hats, there is no question what
becomes of them. They are hung on the

pump-handle, to be gently soaked overnight
with the gentle rain; they float in the bath-tub;
they are brought home tenderly by any kind
friend or faithful servant who may have recognized them in the city park or the village
green; they are reconstructed into foot-balls
and butterfly-traps, and buckets for bailing
mud-puddles. They crown the heads of hob-
goblins made out of broom-sticks and other
available poles. It is easy enough to see what
becomes of the hats.

At noon Little-Breeches is dressed afresh—
clean linen suit, new trousers, shining face,
smooth hair, striped stockings well-gartered
up, new slippers, pansy in his button-hole—
a little stiff with the consciousness of being
well-dressed, but a most appetizing morsel. It
rains, but he has a new pair of rubber boots,
which he is over-anxious to try, and his infat-
uated mother gives him leave to walk to the
barn. To walk to the barn by a roundabout
ramble through the garden seems to him but

a small stretch of privilege, but by the time he
enters the barn his clothes are so thoroughly
damp that when he emerges from the flour-
barrel, into which he entered as his first exploit, he is a mass of paste, and the brave
bright clothes have to be immediately and ig-
nominiously set to soak in the wash-tub, where,
I believe, they remain to this very day.

What can you do? His troubles seem to
come naturally, not wickedly. Even when for
some real and heinous crime he is sent prem-
aturely to bed, he lies and moans, "Oh!
now my heart is broken!" He evidently con-
templates the situation not as punishment, but
as affliction. His busy little brain is all at
sixes and sevens about cause and effect, right
and wrong, sin and suffering.

"Ann," says he, strolling in two hours after
dinner, from which he was missing—"Ann,
have I had my dinner?"

But Ann is non-committal, and says, "How
should I know whether you have had your
dinner or not?"

" Was I at the table, Ann?"

" No, I did not see you at the table."

" Then *of course* I have not had my dinner."

Would you vex this acute little reasoner by forbidding him the dinner he forgot to come home to, and can not even now tell whether he has eaten except by external testimony and abstract argument. *We* take no note of time but from its loss, and he never loses any. Play is his driving and thriving business. School he stoops to — the sturdy, old-fashioned school of books and study and recess — but the city Kindergarten is abomination in his eyes.

" Can I tell Miss Kindergarten "—thus he always calls his teacher, whining most piteously—" can't I tell Miss Kindergarten you want her to let me come home when I feel feeble?" And evidently he has at this moment an overmastering attack of feebleness.

The mature male heart is easily imposed upon.

"Baby-in-Breeches is a frail bud," says papa. "It is too cold and wild for him to go to school to-day," and Little-Breeches rejoices greatly; but in one half-hour the frail bud has vanished from sight, nor appears upon the scene again for three, four, five hours, and then blows in, ruddy, disheveled, shouting, strong, and altogether happy, except for being blown in.

The well-beloved Professor Prophet blesses the house with his presence, and Baby-in-Breeches is warned beforehand that he must not talk at the table. It seems hard to put an interdict on those sweet lips, but, mine own dear little boy, there is no way but this. Baby promises faithfully, and puts on a forty-horse-power pressure of silence. In five minutes— five hours to his waiting and seething soul— he whispers, "Mamma, can't I speak now?"

"No! sh-h!" says mamma.

"Can't I whisper, mamma?"

"No! sh!"

" Mamma," in an ever *crescendo* and start-
lingly audible whisper, " can't I jest tell you
there was a skunk at our school-house to day?
Oh! there was, mamma, and he smelt aw-
fully."

It is a grievous and sore affliction that Baby
can not go to church, and when the tidings
burst upon him that he is to stay at home,
how does he make the powers that be feel
that they are fighting against God by roaring
at the top of his voice, amid strong cryings
and tears, " Oh! I wanted to hear Professor
Prophet's sermon." But because his elders
wish to hear it in peace, and because he would
hear it with multitudinous wrigglings and
twistings and whisperings, with constant and
uncertain down-sittings and up-risings, his soul
is refused that spiritual food, and he remains
ignobly at home. Yet was a better sermon
ever preached than his who called a little
child unto him and said, " Verily I say unto
you, except ye be converted, and become as

little children, ye shall not enter into the kingdom of heaven."

Star-Eyes is so honey-sweet that what seems good in her eyes seems generally most lovely in all other eyes. Can a violet take on tempers? Can a rosebud rage? Can a white lily-cup redden with wrath, or a harebell brew mischief? Then shall Star-Eyes cease to do charming and learn to do evil things. But what if her most dazzling charm be evilspoken of? And yet, when it comes to pattering into my room with a big wet towel, and scrubbing indiscriminately my table and bureau, my vases and baskets, I must demur. I am instinctively certain, moreover, that it is conscience of sin that has brought her to me, and full well she knows such vagaries would not be allowed in the authoritative regions below. How can I mar her innocent enjoyment? But how can I let her irretrievably mar my wares? There is no inherent vice in a wet towel. She is simply exercising her divinely bestowed faculties, expending her beneficently provided surplus energies. How stupid in us not to surround her with objects for which a wet towel has no terrors? How cruel to thwart a human soul in the interests of a senseless piece of furniture! With paint and glass and gilding to create a sin out of a natural and healthy desire! And all the while I am indulging these eminently moral reflections I am meditating an undercurrent of treachery. Taking advantage of a momentary deviation of her thoughts, I surreptitiously seize the towel and drop it down stairs. But Star-Eyes is too quick for me. She sees the tail of the vanishing comet, and laboriously climbs down the stairs, and returns with it triumphant. The process is repeated in all its parts. This will never do. No more cowardly compromise. I must breast the storm. I put the towel on the window-seat beyond reach. She tries to pass me and grasp it. I bar the way. She fails to comprehend the situation; she is slow to un-

derstand that I, her adorer, am really and
steadfastly opposing her will. But the facts
force themselves upon her at last. Then how
splendid is the storm! She knows nor restraint nor repression: only the natural and
full play of feeling. All the rose-leaf face is
flushed with sudden fire. The sunny blue
eyes are aflame with wrath, and down upon
my book descends her little fat hand, charged
with the electric fury of her soul. Then she
is afraid. It is a new experience, and she has
forebodings. As she looks up I see the old
fury and the new fear contending for mastery; and what with her sweetness and her
spirit, and her perfect transparency, I find her
more adorable than ever.

Star-Eyes is going to church. I am ashamed
to mention the motive power which sends her
to take her place in the great congregation. In
the days of our forefathers it would have been
because she was old enough for duty. In
these degenerate days of right-hand fallings-

off and left-hand defections, it is only that some
one has given the small sinner a sash, or a pair
of shoulder - knots, or some other vanity, and
the nurse remarks that Star-Eyes has so many
pretty things it is a pity she should not go to
church — which remark, overheard, perhaps
destined to be overheard by the vain and conceited male mind, results in the fiat that Star
Eyes *shall* go to church. It is not supposed
that she has any " meeting clothes;" but a
resolute nurse gathers together a sufficient
wardrobe, and " nobody is going to take this
girl to church but her father," says the vain
and conceited male mind. So Star Eyes makes
a triumphal entry into church, and sits quietly
snuggled down among the big people—a little folded pink - and - white blossom hidden
among full - blown roses, till a clear, pleasant,
earnest voice suddenly rings through the
church, louder to the ears of her startled parents than the noise of many waters, " Now,
Harry, let Star Eyes take ee fan, and 'oo see
me fan !"

The vain and conceited male mind, brave at home, but cowering before that still, small voice in the church-pew, would fain remove the transgressor, but his cup is not yet full. The young worshiper tolerates the singing and the prayers, but can not yet subdue herself to the sermon. She finds her little cloak more edifying, and amuses herself with vain attempts to put it on. Holding it in front by the two sleeves, she swings it back vigorously over her head, and might effect a lodgment after the twentieth or so trial if a trumpery bonnet on one side, and a big, bare head on the other, did not continually break the force of her swinging. Grown people and their belongings are so terribly in the way! When the cloak is wiled out of her hands, she creeps down upon the floor, and proceeds to investigate the shoes and stockings of the assembly; and, lest she carry her researches into other pews, she is presently and unconsciously lured out of church. Out of church? Not quite so fast.

When half-way down the aisle she suddenly
awakes to a sense of the situation, utters a prolonged shriek of disgust, settles squat on the
floor, utterly refusing to budge, and is swiftly
and succinctly caught up and shot out by a
male mind very much less vain and conceited
than the one that led her in half an hour before.

And now when this poor little demoralized
wretch is put to the torture, and asked, " What
did you do at church ?" she disdains to look up
from doll and tea-set, but answers as she has
been taught, with smiling and self - satisfied
alacrity, " Behaved badly."

Behaved badly.   I suppose so ; but the
church services are never so interesting as
when a baby is pawing and creeping and experimenting around, darting a flash of real life
into the somewhat artificial atmosphere which
envelops us.   In the child we come nearest to
seeing the naked soul.   It is as if we could go
back to the creation and behold how it was

done when He spake. Our theology, strong in its intellectual frame-work, needs ever to be modified and vitalized by fresh and loving observation of life. The Bible is no more a revelation from God than is this little child, and by the one, as surely and pleasantly as by the other, can we learn the divine will and the divine method.

"Papa," says Little-Breeches, radiant with approaching fun—" papa."

" Well."

" No, papa; say ' what.' Papa."

" What ?"

" Nothin'." Tremendous applause.

" Papa," says Star Eyes, in a brilliant encore.

" What ?"

" Nuffin." Yells of delight.

" Little-Breeches," says papa.

" Eh! eh! You can't fool *me!*"

" Star Eyes."

" Nuffin!" And she turns red in the face in her eagerness to prove herself equal to the

U

emergency, nor could all the wit of all the
world more thoroughly "bring down the
house." Little-Breeches thinks we are ap-
plauding his shrewdness, and Star-Eyes has
the ecstatic consciousness of having made a
great hit, and we are all happy.

Yet the little simpletons manage to gather
many scraps of knowledge, if their education
be rather desultory. Few things are talked
about that Baby-in-Breeches does not fasten
upon. in some fragmentary way. He has
picked up the whole of " Barbara Frietche"
long before he can speak intelligibly, but none
the less does he deliver it with head-shaking
energy and true oratorical fervor. Seven-year-
old Muggins has been amused for several even-
ings at bed-time by having repeated to her the
exquisite chorus in Atalanta in Calydon, rep-
resenting the death-scene of Meleager, to
which she has listened with absorbing interest, examining and very satisfactorily compre-
hending it line by line. Little-Breeches is con-

structively in bed and asleep, but really prancing about in his night-gown from *pillow* to post, not to say making occasional raids down stairs. If any thing is safe to say about him, it is safe to say that he does not hear a word of the poetry. But the next morning, waking before Muggins, he bends gently over to see if her eyes are open, and seeing they are not, says softly:

"Who is this bending over thee, lord, with tears and suppression of sighs?"

And I feel very much as if the old Roman Catholic miracle might after all be true, which makes the nine-days-old baby open its mouth and tell who was its father.

Also Muggins, whose taste is omnivorous, delights in that exceptionally charming story of Mrs. Alexander's, "The Wooing o't." "Though it seems to me," she says, just about to fall asleep, "Maggie was very nice and pretty, but I observe that she sewed a great deal. She was always at work on a piece of sewing."

"Never mind," pipes a wee, sleepy voice from under the neighboring bedclothes, "Never mind, Muggins, Trafford loved her all the same." If we are looking at the stars, and trying to pick out and point out the constellations, Little-Breeches is sure next evening that he can "go out and find *the bath-tub*," which is his nomenclature for the Great Dipper— 'tis as like as my fingers to my fingers.

It is time for the children to go home— home into the broad, fresh, blooming country, where they can run and play and breathe and live. The city is too hot and stifling. Even the parks are not safe from the fervid sun by day, and by night there is a perfect shower-bath of children falling out of bed from restlessness. So they are arrayed in spotless dusters, duly furnished with lunch-baskets, and the carriage is at the door. Five-year-old is gradually collected from the balustrade, the back-yards, and the neighbors; Star-Eyes sits up soberly on the back seat, her dear little legs

stuck straight out in front, her soul uplifted
with the dignity of "going on a toot," as she
has somehow learned to call it. Nurse and
Escort depart, well furnished with shawls,
straps, and injunctions.

"And how did you make the journey?" is
eagerly asked when Escort returns.

"Oh, finely. Star-Eyes behaved best of
all."

"And did Little-Breeches keep clean?"

"Clean? Never was such dirtiness seen as
he presented."

"Why *did* not you look out for him?"

"I looked out for his head. That was all I
could do. I could not undertake his clothes."

Of course not. Of course he got at the
lunch-basket before they left the station, and
was eating all the way to New York. He was
constantly making little dabs at the milk-bottle,
and spilling it on the seat. Then he wiped it
up with his sleeve. Then, observing that his
sleeve was wet, he wiped that with the other

sleeve. Dust and cinders very soon finished the business of that jacket. Then there was bread-and-butter to be dropped, and always on the buttered side, and he was ever and anon sitting contemplatively down on pieces of ham, and his pea-nut shells were a grief of heart to the porter, who had to come in and sweep Baby out several times during the journey—but why will they let pea-nuts be peddled through the cars? And so the blessed Baby was safely convoyed home, and rapturously lost within five minutes of being set down at his garden-gate.

THE END.

USEFUL BOOKS FOR FAMILY READING

PUBLISHED BY

HARPER & BROTHERS, NEW YORK.

Either of the following books will be sent by mail, postage prepaid, to any part of the United States, on receipt of price.

HARPER'S NEW MONTHLY MAGAZINE.
49 vols., 8vo, Cloth, $3 00 each; Half Calf, $5 25.

"The Best Monthly Periodical, not in this country alone, but in the English language."—*The Press*, Philadelphia.

HARPER'S WEEKLY. 18 vols., Cloth, $7 00 each; Half Morocco, $10 50.

"A complete Pictorial History of the Times."

HARPER'S BAZAR. A Repository of Fashion, Pleasure, and Instruction. 7 vols., Cloth Gilt, $7 00 each; Half Morocco, $10 50.

"The young lady who buys a single number of HARPER'S BAZAR is made a subscriber for life."—*N. Y. Evening Post*.

ABBOTT'S YOUNG CHRISTIAN SERIES.
The Young Christian Series. By JACOB ABBOTT. Very greatly improved and enlarged. With numerous Engravings. Complete in 4 vols., 12mo, Cloth, $1 75 each.

> THE YOUNG CHRISTIAN.
> THE CORNER STONE.
> THE WAY TO DO GOOD.
> HOARYHEAD AND M'DONNER.

ABBOTT'S CHILD AT HOME. The Child at Home ; or, the Principles of Filial Duty familiarly Illustrated. By JOHN S. C. ABBOTT. Woodcuts. 16mo, Cloth, $1 00.

ABBOTT'S MOTHER AT HOME. The Mother at Home ; or, the Principles of Maternal Duty familiarly Illustrated. By JOHN S. C. ABBOTT. Engravings. 16mo, Cloth, $1 00.

MISS BEECHER'S HOUSEKEEPER AND HEALTHKEEPER : Containing Five Hundred Recipes for Economical and Healthful Cooking ; also, many Directions for securing Health and Happiness. Approved by Physicians of all Classes. Illustrations. 12mo, Cloth, $1 50.

THE TRAINING OF CHILDREN. The Religious Training of Children in the Family, the School, and the Church. By CATHARINE E. BEECHER. 12mo, Cloth, $1 75.

BURTON'S CULTURE OF THE OBSERVING FACULTIES. The Culture of the Observing Faculties in the Family and the School ; or, Things about Home, and how to make them Instructive to the Young. By WARREN BURTON, Author of "The District School as it Was," "Helps to Education," &c. 16mo, Cloth, 75 cents.

BEMENT'S AMERICAN POULTERER'S COMPANION. A Practical Treatise on the Breeding, Rearing, Fattening, and general Management of the various Species of Domestic Poultry. By C. N. BEMENT. Illustrated with Portraits of Fowls, mostly taken from Life ; Poultry-Houses, Coops, Nests, Feeding-Houses, &c., &c. With 120 Illustrations. 12mo, Cloth, $2 00.

COMBE'S TREATISE ON INFANCY. A Treatise on the Physiological and Moral Management of Infancy. For the Use of Parents. By ANDREW COMBE. From the Fourth Edinburgh Edition. 18mo, Cloth, 75 cents.

COMBE'S TREATISE ON DIGESTION. The Physiology of Digestion considered with Relation to the Principles of Dietetics. By ANDREW COMBE. Illustrated. 18mo, Cloth, 75 cents.

COMBE'S PHYSIOLOGY. The Principles of Physiology applied to the Preservation of Health, and the Improvement of Physical and Mental Education. By ANDREW COMBE. With Questions. Engravings. 18mo, Cloth, 75 cents.

DALTON'S PHYSIOLOGY. A Treatise on Physiology and Hygiene ; for Schools, Families and Colleges. By J. C. DALTON, M.D., Professor of Physiology in the College of Physicians and Surgeons, N. Y. With Illustrations. 12mo, Cloth or Half Leather, $1 50.

HOOKER'S CHILD'S BOOK OF NATURE. The Child's Book of Nature, for the Use of Families and Schools; intended to aid Mothers and Teachers in Training Children in the Observation of Nature. In Three Parts. Part I. Plants; Part II. Animals; Part III. Air, Water, Heat, Light, &c. By WORTHINGTON HOOKER, M.D. Engravings. The Three Parts complete in One Volume, Small 4to, Half Roan, $1 60; or, separately, Part I., 60c.; Parts II. and III., 65c. each.

MACE'S PHYSIOLOGY FOR THE YOUNG. The History of a Mouthful of Bread, and its Effect on the Organization of Men and Animals. By JEAN MACÉ. Translated from the Eighth French Edition by Mrs. ALFRED GATTY. 12mo, Cloth, $1 75.

MACE'S PHYSIOLOGY FOR THE YOUNG. The Servants of the Stomach. By JEAN MACÉ, Author of "The History of a Mouthful of Bread," "Home Fairy Tales," &c. Reprinted from the London Edition, Revised and Corrected. 12mo, Cloth, $1 75.

OSGOOD'S AMERICAN LEAVES. American Leaves: Familiar Notes of Thought and Life. By Rev. SAMUEL OSGOOD, D.D. 12mo, Cloth, $1 75.

SMILES'S SELF - HELP. Self-Help; with Illustrations of Character, Conduct, and Perseverance. By SAMUEL SMILES, Author of "The Life of the Stephensons," "The Huguenots," &c. New Edition, Revised and Rewritten. 12mo, Cloth, $1 00.

THE STUDENT'S OLD TESTAMENT HIS-TORY. The Old Testament History. From the Creation to the Return of the Jews from Captivity. Edited by WILLIAM SMITH, LL.D. With Maps and Woodcuts. Large 12mo, Cloth. $2 00.

THE STUDENT'S NEW TESTAMENT HIS-TORY. The New Testament History. With an Introduction, connecting the History of the Old and New Testaments. Edited by WIL-LIAM SMITH, LL.D. With Maps and Woodcuts. 12mo, Cloth, $2 00.

STUDENT'S QUEENS OF ENGLAND. Lives of the Queens of England. From the Norman Conquest. By AGNES STRICKLAND. Abridged by the Author. Revised and Edited by CARO-LINE G. PARKER. 12mo, Cloth, $2 00.

THE STUDENT'S FRANCE. A History of France from the Earliest Times to the Establish-ment of the Second Empire in 1852. Illustrated by Engravings on Wood. Large 12mo, Cloth, $2 00.

THE STUDENT'S HUME. A History of En-gland from the Earliest Times to the Revolution in 1688. By DAVID HUME. Abridged. Incor-porating the Corrections and Researches of re-cent Historians, and continued down to the year 1851. Illustrated by Engravings on Wood. Large 12mo, Cloth, $2 00.

A SMALLER HISTORY OF ENGLAND, from the Earliest Times to the Year 1862. Edited by WILLIAM SMITH, LL.D. Engravings. 16mo, Cloth, $1 00.

THE STUDENT'S GREECE. A History of Greece from the Earliest Times to the Roman Conquest, with Supplementary Chapters on the History of Literature and Art. By WILLIAM SMITH, LL.D. Revised, with an Appendix, by Prof. GEORGE W. GREENE, A.M. Engravings. Large 12mo, Cloth, $2 00.

A SMALLER HISTORY OF GREECE. The above Work abridged for Younger Students and Common Schools. Engravings. 16mo, Cloth, $1 00.

THE STUDENT'S ROME. A History of Rome from the Earliest Times to the Establishment of the Empire. With Chapters on the History of Literature and Art. By HENRY G. LIDDELL, D.D., Oxford. Engravings. Large 12mo, Cloth, $2 00.

A SMALLER HISTORY OF ROME, from the Earliest Times to the Establishment of the Empire. By WILLIAM SMITH, LL.D. With a Continuation to the Fall of the Western Empire in the Year 476. By EUGENE LAWRENCE, A.M. Engravings. 16mo, Cloth, $1 00.

TRACY'S MOTHER AND HER OFFSPRING. The Mother and her Offspring. By STEPHEN TRACY, M.D., formerly Missionary Physician of the A.B.C.F.M. to China. 12mo, Cloth, $1 50.

THE STUDENT'S GIBBON. The History of the Decline and Fall of the Roman Empire. By EDWARD GIBBON. Abridged. Incorporating the Researches of recent Commentators. By WILLIAM SMITH, LL.D. Engravings. Large 12mo, Cloth, $2 00.

VAUX'S ARCHITECTURE. Villas and Cottages: a Series of Designs prepared for Execution in the United States. By CALVERT VAUX, Architect (late DOWNING & VAUX). New Edition, revised and enlarged. Illustrated by nearly 500 Engravings. 8vo, Cloth, $3 00.

WATSON'S AMERICAN HOME GARDEN: being Principles and Rules for the Culture of Vegetables, Fruits, Flowers, and Shrubbery. To which are added brief Notes on Farm Crops, with a Table of their Average Product and Chemical Constituents. By ALEXANDER WATSON. With several Hundred Illustrations. 12mo, Cloth, $2 00.

WEBSTER'S DOMESTIC ECONOMY. Encyclopædia of Domestic Economy: comprising such Subjects as are most immediately connected with Housekeeping; as, the Construction of Domestic Edifices; Articles of Furniture; Animal and Vegetable Substances used as Food, and the Methods of Preserving and Preparing them by Cooking; Making Bread; Materials employed in Dress and the Toilet; Business of the Laundry; Preservation of Health; Domestic Medicine, &c. By THOMAS WEBSTER. With Additions by an American Physician. With nearly 1000 Engravings. 8vo, Sheep, $5 00.

THE BAZAR BOOK OF DECORUM. The Care of the Person, Manners, Etiquette, and Ceremonials.   16mo, Cloth, $1 00.

THE BAZAR BOOK OF HEALTH. The Dwelling, the Nursery, the Bedroom, the Dining Room, the Parlor, the Library, the Kitchen, the Sick-Room.   16mo, Cloth, $1 00.

SMILES'S CHARACTER. Character. By SAMUEL SMILES, Author of "Self-Help," "History of the Huguenots," "Life of the Stephensons," &c.   12mo, Cloth, $1 50.

JACOB ABBOTT ON TRAINING THE YOUNG. Gentle Measures in the Management and Training of the Young. A Book for the Parents of Young Children. By JACOB ABBOTT.   Illustrated.   12mo, Cloth, $1 75.

ABBOTT'S SCIENCE FOR THE YOUNG. Science for the Young. By JACOB ABBOTT. Illustrated.

    Vol. I. HEAT.   12mo, Cloth, $1 50.

    Vol. II. LIGHT.   12mo, Cloth, $1 50.

    Vol. III. WATER AND LAND.   12mo, Cloth, $1 50.

    Vol. IV. FORCE.   12mo, Cloth, $1 50.